A balloonist's assistant
takes Ki for a ride

The big bag above them seemed to lean to one side, then the leaning movement became a sudden sharp jump. The basket began swaying and, without warning, tilted sharply as the bag suddenly swirled in a three-quarter turn.

Nora was still half-kneeling above the chemical container, and the basket's sudden tilting swirl caught her off-balance and tossed her sidewise. Ki released his grip on the basket's rim and dived for her, trying to keep her from falling. Nora's weight pulled him down with her to the bottom of the swaying, tossing basket. They landed and slid until they reached the basket's side, where they lay sprawled in a curled tangle of arms and legs.

"We'd better just lie still until the basket stops," she told Ki.

"I can stand it if you can," Ki replied.

"I don't mind it," she said quickly. "This isn't the first time I've been pinned under..."

— WESLEY ELLIS —

LONE STAR

AND THE
CON MAN'S RANSOM

J®

A JOVE BOOK

LONE STAR AND THE CON MAN'S RANSOM

A Jove Book/published by arrangement with
the author

PRINTING HISTORY
Jove edition/December 1986

ISBN: 0-515-08797-1

Jove Books are published by the Berkley Publishing Group,
200 Madison Avenue, New York, N.Y. 10016. The words
"A JOVE BOOK" and the "J" with sunburst are trademarks
belonging to Jove Publications, Inc.

PRINTED IN THE UNITED STATES OF AMERICA

Chapter 1

"It's a good feeling, not having to worry about the cartel anymore," Jessie told Ki.

They were riding across the vast unfenced grazing range that formed the southwestern area of the Circle Star. Because it was the most isolated part of the ranch, and provided the scantest grass, the hands called it "the Desert." Jessie hadn't taken her eyes off the terrain ahead when she spoke, and now she touched Sun's flank with the toe of her boot to avoid a gully that opened just ahead of them.

"Yes." Ki nodded. He reined his own mount to follow Jessie's shift in direction. "But it's a feeling I'm having a little trouble getting used to."

"Oh, so am I. I was just thinking, this is the first year we've been able to go to the after-roundup barbecue since it was our turn to have it at the Circle Star. That was three years ago, and I've missed keeping in touch with our neighbors."

"It hasn't been because we've wasted time," Ki said. "And at least we won't have the interruptions that took up so much of our time before the cartel was smashed."

"I was thinking that myself." Jessie nodded. "It's been a long fight, Ki, but it doesn't look as though we'll be in a state of constant warfare any longer. I'll enjoy being able

1

to visit with Brad and George Brady and Bob Manners again."

Each year, the Circle Star and the three adjoining ranches that shared common boundaries with the Starbuck spread on the sprawling Southwest Texas range followed the cattleman's tradition of holding a come-one, come-all barbecue between the end of the roundup and the beginning of the trail drives that took their cattle to market. A different ranch hosted the barbecue each year, and this year's host was the Cross Spikes, which lay to the southwest of the Starbuck range.

Because the Circle Star wranglers had gone a long time without a holiday, Jessie had told them to get an early start. Most of the cowhands had ridden off before sunrise, as soon as they'd finished breakfast, and the others had followed soon afterward.

Jessie and Ki had stayed behind while Jessie dealt with the mail that one of the hands had brought in from the railroad depot late the previous day. As usual following the end of a month, the mail had been heavier than usual, with reports from the far-flung Starbuck enterprises.

"Maybe we'd better move a little faster, if we don't want to get soaked before we get to the Cross Spikes," Ki suggested, pointing to the billowing gray clouds that were beginning to form a threatening line just ahead of them. "I'd say that's a spring thundershower taking shape."

"It certainly looks like it," Jessie agreed. "And I came away without my slicker."

"So did I," Ki confessed. "But it won't be the first time either one of us has been caught and gotten wet."

"I don't mind it a bit at this time of year. Besides, we need it to keep the water holes filled."

Jessie touched Sun's flank with her booted foot, and the

magnificent palomino stallion picked up his pace. Ki followed suit, and they rode on in companionable silence toward the gathering cloudbank. Ahead of them, a small herd of cattle was beginning to bunch as the beasts' instincts warned them of the approaching weather change.

Jessie reined Sun onto a slanted course that would take them past the herd at a distance great enough to avoid disturbing the cattle, still restless from the chousing they'd taken during the roundup. Again, Ki followed suit.

Both he and Jessie were studying the gathering clouds as they rode. On the prairie in this part of Texas, weather was seldom predictable. Though the eastern boundary of the Circle Star was a bit more than a hundred miles from the Gulf of Mexico, a major weather disturbance above its always restless waters could send roiling rain clouds scudding at an unbelievably fast speed across the level, featureless terrain.

Heavy with the warm moisture they'd sucked up from the Gulf, the clouds dropped their load in sheets when they collided with the cooler air currents moving toward them from the heights of the Edwards Plateau, which marked the end of the level prairie with its big cattle spreads.

"If it does rain, it won't last long," Ki said as a glare of sheet lightning flashed behind the cloudbank.

"No," Jessie agreed. "And if we do get wet, I'll just think about all those water holes the storm will fill."

"Water's better than money in the bank to any ranch in this part of the country," Ki agreed.

"Maybe you shouldn't have mentioned money, Ki," Jessie said with a smile. Then the smile faded as she went on, "It reminded me of something we need to talk about."

"Now's as good a time as any," Ki suggested.

"I suppose so. I'm a bit worried—" Jessie broke off

3

abruptly when a bolt of lightning blinded them as it shot down from the clouds that hung low above the prairie just ahead.

While they talked, Jessie and Ki had gotten very close to the small scattered herd of longhorns. The clap of thunder and the flash of the lightning bolt had spooked the range-wild steers. They were tossing their heads now, blatting and milling, and suddenly one of them on the perimeter of the herd cut away from its fellows with a wild, throaty snorting and charged Ki's horse. The animal was only a dozen yards away, heading for Ki from behind, when Jessie saw it.

"Look out, Ki!" she cried, yanking hard at Sun's reins to turn the palomino and give Ki room to spur past her.

Ki had been riding in his usual relaxed manner, his attention on Jessie. Even his quick reaction was not as fast as that of his mount. The horse's inborn instinct to the threat of the onrushing steer was to whirl instantly and buck away from the longhorn's charge. Expert rider though he was, Ki's response was a split second behind that of the horse. Arms waving, he was tossed out of his saddle.

Somersaulting in midair, Ki landed on his feet and whirled aside in the fraction of a second before the wide-spread swinging horns of the panicked steer caught him. The needle-sharp tip of one horn grazed Ki's chest as he threw himself backward in a leaping spring that left the steer charging through empty air.

Sun's quick leap took Jessie to Ki's side. She reached out an arm. Ki grabbed her hand with one of his, swung toward her, and caught the saddlehorn with his free hand. Sun completed his fast, surefooted sidewise swing, and the big palomino's turn lifted Ki above the longhorn's next swiveling charge. The steer's lunge carried it beyond the palomino's side, and by that time Jessie was nudging Sun's flank with her heels. The long, fast stride of the big golden horse took them to one side of the longhorn, which plunged straight ahead until it reached the milling herd and stopped, still swinging its big head and snorting angrily.

Jessie had managed to keep a firm grasp on the reins with one hand. She tugged to turn Sun in the direction of Ki's pony. For the few seconds that passed before they reached the riderless pony, Ki dangled in midair. Jessie reined and Ki dropped to the ground only a long step away from his mount. He regained the saddle of the cow pony before the longhorn herd had time to react.

In spite of their menacing appearance, the lowering clouds released only a few scattered drops, not enough even to be called a shower. Swirling currents in the upper air were already carrying the cloudbank beyond Jessie and Ki by the time Ki had regained his saddle.

"I never did really believe the old range story about cattle refusing to charge a man on horseback," he said to Jessie as they came within easy speaking distance.

"Longhorns are as unpredictable as humans," she replied with a smile. "But we are lucky, at that."

"I think Sun gets most of the credit," Ki told her. "I'd say he's earned an extra ration of oats today."

"He has, and I'll see that he gets it," she said.

"Now, what was it you were about to tell me when that little dustup started?" Ki asked. "Something that I said about money had reminded you of it."

"Yes." She nodded. "I'm worried about the Silver City mine, Ki. It's been producing less and less silver for the past several months, and I'm wondering if the lode's going to be worth working very much longer."

"We both know how unpredictable those silver lodes can be," Ki said thoughtfully. "They'll slack off in production when the ore deposits are thinner, then after a few months they'll get back to good production again."

"That hasn't been true of the Silver City mine, though," Jessie said. Frowning now, she went on, "From the beginning it's been a very steady producer. What makes me suspicious is that while the monthly reports show the mine's silver output is dropping, the copper production stays the same."

Now a frown began to grow on Ki's face. He knew as well as Jessie did that in any silver-ore deposit in the world a mine produced both silver and copper at a constant ratio between the two metals. He said, "That's certainly not normal. Do you think Coats is stealing silver?"

"Either Coats or somebody working in the office there," she said. "But even if it isn't Coats himself, I'll have to fire him anyhow."

"Why, if he's not the thief?"

"He might be as honest as his recommendations said he was when I hired him, Ki. But if he hasn't noticed that somebody is stealing silver from the mine, he's not competent to manage it."

"You're thinking about going to Silver City, then?"

"I think we'll have to," Jessie replied. "I'd have suggested that we go after looking at last month's report from the mine, but I didn't want to leave with the roundup just starting. I can't just act on suspicions, Ki. I've got to see for myself what's happening there before I'll know how to cure it. If Dan Coats is the one who's stealing the silver, I want to get him away from the mine as soon as possible."

"I agree." Ki nodded. "It's not too much of a trip to Silver City. We ought to be able to make it and be back here at the Circle Star before the men start forming the market herd."

"Three weeks or so," Jessie said. "Just a quick trip to Silver City and back. Yes, that's about right."

"Then I suppose we'll leave tomorrow or the next day?"

"As soon as we can, yes."

"I'll be thinking about the little odd jobs that have to be done before we leave, then."

"Good. So will I. And won't it be nice to be able to take our time instead of having to hurry away to stop some sort of brushfire the cartel lighted?"

"At least it'll be something new."

"That's how I feel, too. Now, let's forget about what we have to do in the future and enjoy the Cross Spikes barbecue."

Though their boundary fences made neighbors of the Box B, the Lazy G, the Cross Spikes, and the Circle Star, their headquarters houses were miles apart. By the time Jessie and Ki got to the headquarters of the Cross Spikes, the barbecue was well under way.

At a little distance from the main house improvised trestle tables made a rough semicircle around the big barbecue pit. It had been opened long enough for about half the cowhands to be served, and many of the tables were occupied by men from all four of the spreads, digging into big slabs of beef, bowls of pinto beans, pickles and sliced onions, and platters piled high with freshly baked bread. The smell of spicy barbecue sauce and the chatter of talk from the hands still waiting to be served filled the air.

At one side of the barbecue pit, George Brady stood talking with Brad Close, owner of the Box B, and Bob Manners of the Lazy G. They were honoring one of the unwritten rules of a ranch barbecue, that all the cowhands be served before the owners started eating. Far enough away from the tables to be undisturbed by the occasionally rough language of the chattering hands, and looking a bit out of place as the only women in the crowd, Nettie Brady and Samantha Manners stood close together.

"I'd better join the ladies as soon as I've said hello to Brad and George and Bob," Jessie told Ki as they dismounted at the rope picket line where the horses were tethered. "Go ahead and join the others. We'll have plenty of time to talk on the way home and decide about our trip to Silver City."

With a nod, Ki started toward the barbecue pit while Jessie angled across to where the ranch owners were standing.

"Well, Jessie!" Brad Close called as she drew near the three men. "It's taken you so long to get here, we was just wondering whether you was coming when we seen you riding up."

"We got a late start," Jessie said. "Then on the way we had a little run-in with one of those half-wild longhorns I've added to my herd."

"Those longhorns spook awful easy," Brady put in as Jessie turned to offer her hand to him after Close released it. "But better late than not at all. Real glad to see you, Jessie."

"And so am I," Manners said as he also shook Jessie's hand. "Since we're talking about longhorns, you mind telling me how the ones you've got are shaping up?"

"Pretty well, I'd say," she replied. "I'll be able to tell you more about them in a few months."

"I was halfway figuring a while back to see how they'd do here on the Cross Spikes," Brady went on. "But I decided to stick with Herefords."

"Now, I'm thinking real strong about trying out some of the Brahma crosses that they're developing down at the King Ranch," Bob Manners said. "Any of you heard how they're doing this far from that wet coastal range?"

"I don't think there's enough of them off the King

8

Ranch yet for anybody to make a judgment," Brady replied.

"And I've been gone too much to keep abreast of all the new breeds they're developing," Jessie admitted. "But Ki and I will be staying closer to home now—at least that's what I plan."

"Well, that'll be nice," Brad Close put in. "Maybe you and me will have a chance to visit a little bit more, now."

"I'll hold you to that," Jessie told her old friend, then turned to Brady and Manners and added, "And I hope I'll see you more often at the Circle Star, too. Now, I think I'd better go over and have a little bit of woman-talk with the other ladies. With only three of us, we're such a minority that we've got to stick together to keep all you men in line."

"I don't know about George"—Manners smiled—"but Samantha doesn't give me much loose rope."

"Nettie's the same with me," Brady said quickly.

"You fellows are lucky to have somebody to keep a rein on you," Close put in. "There ain't nothing like a wife to keep a man company and see he don't get into mischief."

With a final smile at her neighbors, Jessie started toward the two women. Although she was much younger than either of them, the isolation of ranch life gave the women a common bond. In an area where each steer required a hundred acres of range for grazing, the spreads were necessarily so big that visits between neighboring ranches were few and far between. They chatted easily together, watching the waiting cowhands move up to the barbecue pit to be served.

At last the final cowhand held his plate to be heaped up with the spicy beef and started toward the tables. Jessie and her companions moved toward the spot where Brady, Manners, and Close still stood talking.

9

"Now, George and Bob's got ladies to look after," Brad Close told Jessie as they started toward the barbecue pit. "So I guess you're stuck with me to look after you."

"I can't think of anything I'd enjoy more," Jessie replied. "It'll be nice to talk, Brad. We've seen too little of each other lately."

"Maybe that won't be the case now, since you said you was going to stay closer to the Circle Star," Close suggested.

"It won't be. Ki and I may have one more short trip to make in a few days, up into New Mexico, but we'll be able to settle down after that."

"Then I'll be visiting with you," the old rancher promised.

Their plates filled, Jessie and Close followed the other owners to a small table set near the center of the semicircle formed by those where the hands were still eating. They were silent for a while after passing the bowls of beans and relishes around, saying little while they concentrated on the richly seasoned meat and crusty bread.

No one in the group at the owners' table really noticed the change that took place in the tables occupied by the cowhands until the noisy chattering that had filled the air began to fade into silence. Jessie was the first to look around. She saw the tanned faces of the cowhands turning up and only then became aware of the silence that was falling over the crowd. Her eyes went up, she gasped, then like the wranglers at the other tables she stopped chewing and stared.

Outlined against the sky, now bright blue and without a cloud, she saw the round shape of a balloon, its basket dangling and swaying beneath it as the currents in the upper air carried it steadily toward the spot where the tables stood. Then one of the cowhands called out loudly and broke the sudden silence.

"Hey!" the wrangler cried. "It's a balloon, and it looks to me like it's starting to come down!"

His shout broke the spell of silence and a noisy gabble of chatter filled the air. Most of the cowhands were on their feet by now, food forgotten as they stared at the balloon and its dangling basket swaying below it. The aircraft was close enough now to see the silhouetted form of a man in the basket. He began waving as the balloon dropped slowly but steadily to the ground.

"Where the devil could that have come from?" Bob Manners exclaimed. "There wasn't anything up there just a few minutes ago when I glanced up to see what time it was getting to be!"

"I imagine there's a lot more wind up there than we're getting down here on the ground," Brady said. "And that cowhand was right—it *is* coming down. Looks like it'll land real close to the main house if it keeps on dropping the way it is now."

The cowboys were leaving the tables now, running back and forth, trying to find a spot where the balloon would pass directly over their heads. All of them seemed to be talking at the same time, and the result was a babble of voices in which none of the chatter could be understood.

By now, Jessie could see quite clearly that at the slower rate the balloon was dropping it would reach earth much farther from the ranch house than Brady had estimated. She looked around for the Cross Spikes owner, saw he'd moved with the flow of the group trying to get directly below the balloon's path, and worked her way to where he was standing. Brady's head was thrown back, his eyes following the course of the slow-moving balloon.

"That balloon's not coming down as fast as it was when we first saw it, George," she said. "Do you have any cattle on the range in the direction it's moving?"

"I sure do! It's heading for the fenced range where I run my breeding stock."

"Don't you think a few of your hands had better ride under it? You know how cattle panic when they see something new."

"That's just what I was beginning to think." Brady nodded. "I think I'll go along with them myself, too."

"Do you mind if I join you? It's not every day we see a balloon around here. I'd like to get a close look at it."

"Come along and welcome, Jessie. I don't imagine you'll be the only one who's interested."

Jessie and Brady started toward the corral, and before they'd reached it a dozen others had broken from the crowd and joined them. Within minutes a band of almost twenty Cross Spikes hands and guests were mounted and riding in a straggling line, hurrying to catch up with the slowly descending balloon before it reached the ground.

Chapter 2

Pursuit of the balloon was easy over the flat, featureless prairie, and though it had sailed past the ranch house the crowd following it had no trouble catching up.

Soon after they'd started, Jessie saw Ki riding up to her. He came alongside and matched the gait of his horse to Sun's, then asked, "Why are we doing this, Jessie? That balloon could sail on for a long way, even if it is pretty low right now."

"I hadn't thought about it that way, Ki. I think everybody just got the same idea at once, mounted up, and began riding."

"Well, I don't have any objection to joining the crowd," Ki went on. "I just got to wondering and thought you might have an idea why we're chasing after it."

"For one thing, George and I were concerned the cattle might panic if the balloon came down among them. Besides that, Ki, you've got to admit that in this part of the country a balloon sailing overhead isn't something that happens every day."

"Of course it isn't. And I suppose I'm as curious as everyone else to find out where it came from and what it's doing here."

"We ought to know pretty soon," Jessie said. She

13

pointed to the balloon. Ki lifted his eyes to follow her gesture and she went on, "It looks to me like it's getting lower a little faster than it was when we first noticed it."

"Yes, it is," Ki agreed. "So I suppose our curiosity will be satisfied pretty quickly."

When the balloon had first been sighted, it was at least two hundred feet above the ground. Now it was less than half that height, and was moving forward more and more slowly as it dropped through the windless surface air. The crowd of riders pursuing the aircraft had strung out during their chase. Jessie glanced back and saw that she and Ki were now part of a winding, snakelike line that was at least a mile long. She looked ahead again and saw that the balloon was still losing altitude. It was now only thirty or forty feet up. Its forward movement had almost stopped.

"We should get to it just about the time it touches the ground," Ki commented as they rode ahead. "I hope whoever that fellow in the basket is knows what to do when he hits. It seems to me that's the most dangerous part of going up in one of those things."

"I'm sure he'll be able to handle it," Jessie replied. "If he didn't know how to land, I don't imagine he'd have gone up in the first place."

"Well, that makes sense," Ki agreed. "And if he needs any help, he'll certainly have enough. Those cowhands in front of us are pulling up. They must have seen he's about to come down."

Almost before Ki stopped talking the balloon began to drop more rapidly. The man in the basket was waving again now, gesturing to the riders immediately below to follow him. Almost to a man they dismounted and started running after the aircraft.

By now the balloon was stationary, the bottom of its basket only fifteen feet or so above the heads of the men

14

below, and Jessie and Ki could see the balloonist tossing out coils of rope that uncoiled as they dropped. The cowhands were running to catch the ropes, crowding and jostling in their excitement and eagerness to help bring the craft to earth.

After they'd covered the next few yards, Jessie and Kit could hear the balloonist's voice clearly. He was shouting to his volunteer helpers, giving them instructions.

"You men keep an eye on each other," he called. "Try to keep those ropes the same length! If you pull too hard on one side or the other you might upset the basket, and I'm still high enough to break my neck if I get thrown out!"

For a moment it appeared that the aeronaut's warning of a fall might come about. In their enthusiasm, some of the men on the ground were hauling in line too fast, and the basket tilted dangerously. The less excited hands in the amateur ground crew saw the danger in time and yelled at their fellows, while the man in the basket clung to one of the shrouds that supported the bag until the moment of danger had passed.

Jessie and Ki reined in and dismounted just as the bottom of the basket touched the ground. Then there was another flurry of excitement when some of the rope-holders released their grip and the basket again tilted dangerously to one side.

"Don't let go of the ropes!" the aeronaut shouted. "We've got to anchor this bag until I let more of the air escape!"

"Anchor it to what?" one of the helpers called, his voice raised as though the balloon were still soaring high above him.

"Rocks, trees, bushes, anything you can find to anchor it to!" the balloonist replied.

"Mister, there ain't a damn thing but dry dirt around

15

here!" another of the wranglers said. "But don't worry, we'll hang on till you tell us to turn your contraption loose."

"You won't have to hold on very long," the aeronaut said reassuringly. "I'm almost out of lift now. Another few minutes, and you can let go."

By now Jessie and Ki had walked up to the edge of the crowd of cowhands holding the ropes. Jessie looked curiously at the aeronaut, who was still in the basket, tugging at a cord that ran up from the basket through the dangling fabric of a spoutlike nozzle at the bottom of the air bag. Jessie could not repress a grin when she looked at the bag and its appendage. She turned to Ki to tell him the thought that had occurred to him.

Ki was grinning as widely as she was, and she asked, "Are you thinking what I am?"

"You say it first," Ki replied. "I'll tell you if you're right."

"From where we're standing, that balloon looks like a cow with only one teat," Jessie went on.

"Exactly," Ki chuckled. "And if I'm not imagining things, it's shrinking all the time."

Creases were forming now in the sleek, shiny surface of the balloon's bag, and the man in the cockpit was moving from one shroud to the next, tugging at the ropes experimentally. Jessie tried to get a glimpse of his face, but he was moving with his back toward her, and when he turned she saw that he was wearing goggles and a close-fitting leather helmet. All she could see was the tip of his nose and his mouth. Under the helmet and goggles he had on a sort of loose coverall with long sleeves buttoned tightly at his wrists, a costume that effectively concealed both his face and his body.

"Give it another five minutes," he said to the group of

16

his volunteer helpers. "It's losing lift faster now."

"Is hot air all that keeps this contrivance up in the air?" one of the cowhands asked.

"That's all. As long as the air inside the bag is warmer than the air outside, it'll float right along," the man in the basket replied.

"Seems to me like a man could go clear to heaven if he was to pick out the right day for it," another of the hands said thoughtfully.

"You better not let a preacher hear you talk like that," one of the others put in. "He'd have you down on your prayer-bones for a month afterwards."

"Well, I don't guess it'd hurt me none. By the time I've put in the kinda day's work the foreman looks for me to, I ain't got much time left to do a lot of praying."

"Now, boys, let's don't start talking about religion," George Brady said. "Just act like you would in the bunk-house."

On most ranches, there was a strict rule against the hands discussing religion. Over the years, the owners and foremen had learned that religious discussions often started fights, and had barred the controversial topic of churches and creeds from bunkhouse conversation.

Brady went on, now addressing the balloonist. "What I'd sure like to know is how far you've traveled today in that contraption of yours."

"How far is it from here to the railroad?" the man in the basket asked.

"Right at fifteen miles," one of the hands volunteered.

"I left the tracks at noon," the aeronaut said.

"But that's not two hours ago!" Brady protested. "It takes me longer than that to get there on a horse!"

"Mister, balloons are going to put horses out of style in a few more years," the balloonist said. "All we've got left

17

to do is to figure out some way to push 'em against the wind." He stopped short and began tugging at the shrouds once more, then called to his volunteer helpers, "I think the bag's slack enough now. Stand clear while I toss out my anchor."

In a moment, a three-pronged iron hook attached to a rope, more a grapnel than an anchor, sailed out of the basket. It slid slowly along the ground until two of the curved points dug into the hard soil. The rope grew taut, the anchor slipped a few feet, then the points dug in again, and the balloon came to a halt.

As soon as it had stopped, the watching cowhands surged toward it like a tide, forming a rough circle around the basket and the balloon itself, now sagging down like a mushroom.

"You men look all you want to," the aeronaut said as he levered himself over the edge of the basket and dropped to the ground. "Just don't bother anything. If you want to ask me any questions, I'll be glad to answer them in a minute." Looking around, he located Brady in the crowd and started toward him. "You acted like you're in charge here," he said.

"I guess I did." Brady nodded. "It happens that you've landed on my ranch. My name's Brady, George Brady." As the two men shook hands, Jessie came up. Brady went on, "This is Miss Jessica Starbuck. She owns the spread right next to mine."

"Glad to meet you, ma'am," the aeronaut said. "And you, too, Mr. Brady." He was tugging at the chin strap of his helmet as he spoke. "I'm Ted Sanders. I don't guess I need to tell you what line of work I'm in," he went on, nodding toward the balloon. "And I hope you don't mind me coming to earth on your land."

18

"I'm glad you did," Brady replied. "We don't have this kind of excitement very often."

"I won't be staying very long, but I'll have to wait for my crew to get here. They've been following me in a wagon, and I got a little ahead of them. That's why I decided to land."

Sanders had his helmet off by now, and Jessie studied his face with interest. He was a young man, clean-shaven, with blue eyes and reddish-blond hair. She guessed him to be in his middle twenties, judging by his lithe walk and the easy way he'd leaped from the basket, but creases at the corners of his eyes and wrinkle lines in his high forehead made him look older.

"You've got quite a crowd here," Sanders said. "From what I saw when I sailed over, it looks like you're having a big picnic. Do all these people work for you?"

"Oh, no," Brady replied. "Some are my hands, of course, but most of them are from the other ranches close by. We have a sorta blowout every year after roundup. That's why there's so many of us."

"I see. Well, I don't suppose you'll object to my keeping the balloon here while I wait for my wagon? As soon as it gets here, we'll load the bag on it and go about our business."

"Leave it as long as you like, Sanders." The rancher was looking around the crowd. "Jessie," he went on, "why don't you visit with Mr. Sanders while I go look for Brad and Bob?"

As Brady left, Jessie asked Sanders, "Do you mind telling me why you're having to wait for a wagon? Can't you just put some more hot air in the balloon and float off again?"

"I could do that, of course." Sanders nodded. "And I'd

19

get to where I was going a lot faster, as well as having an easier ride. But I've learned what I wanted to find out, so I didn't see any use in staying up any longer."

"It's not any of my business, of course," Jessie said. "But I'm curious about what you were trying to find out. Would you mind telling me?"

"As a matter of fact, Miss Starbuck, I'd like nothing better than to tell you. I'm working on an idea."

Sanders stopped short, and though Jessie expected him to pick up his explanation, he seemed lost in thought. "I still haven't heard what you're looking for," she prompted him.

"Oh!" he exclaimed. "I'm sorry. I stopped to think about how I could answer your question."

"Just start at the beginning and go on," she suggested.

"Well, I've got some ideas that a lot of people think are a little bit crazy. I'm trying to learn how to turn ballooning into a business, instead of just a stunt that's used to attract a crowd to a circus or carnival."

A puzzled frown grew on Jessie's face as the aeronaut stopped again. She asked him, "What kind of business could you possibly make out of a balloon?"

"Before I answer, let me ask you a question, Miss Starbuck. Have you ever been up in a balloon?"

Jessie shook her head as she said, "No. And to tell you the truth, I've never even thought about going up in one."

"You should. You'd be surprised how much you can see when you're a few hundred feet up in the air. Now, Mr. Brady said you own a ranch somewhere close by."

"Yes. George and I are neighbors. My ranch is the Circle Star. It's just northeast of here."

"There's a fence between your ranch and his, I suppose?"

20

"I can see you're a stranger to cattle ranching, Mr. Sanders," Jessie said. "Certainly there's a fence. Quite a few fences, in fact. All the spreads here are fenced around the boundary lines, and there are other fences on them to keep different herds separated, and to close in the nursery range—that's where the mother cows and their calves are kept. Roundups would be a nightmare without fences, Mr. Sanders."

"Yes, I remember seeing quite a few stretches of barbed wire while I was floating this way," Sanders said. "And I suppose the cattle break through them occasionally?"

"Yes, certainly they do. Of course, on the Circle Star, I have two or three hands working on fences almost all the time."

"Riding horseback from one to the other, of course?"

"Of course. How else would they get around? This is level country, and there aren't many trees, but it's too broken up to make carts or buggies practical."

"Horseback is slow, Miss Starbuck. In my balloon, I could soar over your entire ranch and in about two hours I'd find all the places where your fences needed attention. Then your men wouldn't have to waste time looking for breaks."

"Yes, I suppose that's true. And there are times when we have cattle break a boundary fence and stray. I'm sure you can see farther in a balloon than you can from a saddle."

"A man on horseback can see about seven miles in level country like this," Sanders said. "I've done a little studying on the subject. A hundred feet off the ground in my balloon, I can see seventy miles on a clear day. If I go high enough, I can see seven hundred miles."

"But you wouldn't be able to see broken fences or

21

strayed cattle that high up!" Jessie protested.

"Oh, I'd take a spyglass up with me," he replied. "And—"

Their conversation was interrupted by Brady's return. He'd brought Brad Close and Bob Manners with him.

After introductions were completed, Jessie said, "Mr. Sanders has been telling me some of his ideas about using his balloon on ranches instead of having our hands do chores like riding fences and keeping our herds shaped up. I was really quite fascinated by his ideas."

"If they sounded good to you, I guess all of us would be interested, Jessie," Brad Close said.

"I'm sure we would," Brady agreed. "But let's don't forget about the barbecue. A lot of us got pulled away before we were through eating." He turned to Sanders. "Why don't you come back to the main house with us, and we'll listen to your schemes while we finish? I'd imagine you could use a bite yourself."

"I can't leave my balloon," Sanders replied. "But thanks just the same."

"Suppose I leave a couple of my hands to keep an eye on it," Brady suggested. "I can find a man or two who's had his fill and won't mind staying."

"That'll be fine, as long as they promise to keep their hands off my balloon," Sanders agreed.

"They will. And it'll give us a chance to talk more about your ideas. Even if we don't take to them, you're not going to be turned away without a hearing."

With Sanders riding the horse of one of the cowhands who stayed to watch the balloon, they returned to the barbecue pit and replenished their plates. The aeronaut launched into an exposition of his ideas at once. They were many and varied, and included aerial mapping and surveying, transporting lightweight merchandise faster than a railroad could do the job, weather watching, and several more.

Jessie and the other ranch owners listened to him with a kind of skeptical fascination, and when he'd at last fallen silent, Jessie asked the first question that had popped into her mind. "How can you possibly do all these things you've been talking about, Mr. Sanders, when your balloon only goes where the wind takes it?"

"That's not quite accurate, Miss Starbuck. You're making the assumption a lot of folks make. Upper-air currents are like a layer cake. There may be a south wind a hundred feet above the ground, a north wind at a hundred and fifty feet, and one blowing east or west at two hundred feet. It's usually possible to change the direction of a balloon just by going higher or dropping lower."

"And you can go higher or lower if you want to?"

"Certainly."

"How?" Jessie persisted.

"Two ways, Miss Starbuck. I carry a half-dozen bags of sand or dirt on the outside of the basket, and when I empty one or two the balloon goes higher because it's lifting a lighter load. But that's not all. I have a calcium chloride cylinder that produces hydrogen gas when I dampen the chemical with a few drops of water. The hot vapor goes up into the bag and the balloon starts lifting."

"Now, I never heard of that!" Brady exclaimed. "What about going lower? I guess you just let out some hot air?"

"Exactly, Mr. Brady. It's called venting, and you saw me doing it when I landed on the prairie a while ago."

"Well, I guess your scheme might work the way you say it will," Brad Close said. "But I'm too old and set in my ways to feel like trying it. Jessie and George and Bob might want to, but you can count me out."

"I think I'll pass, too," Bob Manners said quickly. "It

sounds good when you talk about it, but I'd rather have a man on a horse going out than somebody up in the air a hundred feet."

"I'm afraid I've got to agree," said Brady. "We're doing pretty well the way things are now. I'd just as lief keep 'em that way."

"How about you, Miss Starbuck?" Sanders asked, trying to keep his disappointment from showing in his voice.

"I'd want to think about it a while," Jessie replied. "But I remember how my father did well in his shipping line by switching from wooden ships to iron hulls before most of his competitors did. And I also remember how many times he told me never to be afraid to try a new idea."

"Then you'll give me a chance to show you I can do what I've been telling you about?" Sanders' voice was vibrant with hope.

"I told you, I'll have to think about it," Jessie answered calmly. "But if you want to bring your balloon to the Circle Star, I'll give you a chance to show me that you can do what you say."

"That's all I want!" the aeronaut said. "But I'd better tell you that I have two assistants who'll be going with me. Tim O'Brien is one of the best aeronauts in the world, and his daughter Nora is almost as good as I am. They should be showing up any minute with the wagon."

"We have plenty of room," Jessie told him. "And I'm sure you'll need their help."

"I'd get along by myself, but it's going to be easier with Tim and Nora there," Sanders replied. "And as soon as they get here with the wagon, I'll haul the balloon over to your ranch and give you any kind of demonstration you ask for!"

24

Chapter 3

"You're sure you're not nervous, Miss Starbuck?" Ted Sanders asked Jessie.

"I suppose I am, and just don't want to admit it," she confessed. "I've never been up in a balloon before."

"Very few people have," Sanders said encouragingly. "But you don't have a thing to worry about."

Jessie and the aeronaut were standing beside the basket, the bag of the balloon rising above them. The spot Sanders had chosen for the ascension was the cripple pasture just beyond the Circle Star's corral, and behind the corral bars the horses had been whinnying nervously since the globe of the balloon began puffing up. The cowhands who weren't riding fences, tallying pastures, or doing other range chores stood between the cookshack and the bunkhouse, watching the preparations, and Ki was just coming out of the main house.

Sections of stovepipe stretched from one side of the balloon basket a half-dozen yards from the dangling spout of the bag to the fire tended by Sanders' helpers. The stovepipe ended in a sheet-iron hood held by stakes above an almost smokeless mesquite-wood blaze from which shimmering heat waves were rising.

On opposite sides of the hood, Timothy O'Brien and his

daughter Nora divided their attention between the fire and the bulging balloon. Most of the wrinkles were out of the big bag's slick fabric now, and the balloon was already buoyant. The basket had risen a few inches off the ground and was tugging at the rope that held it anchored.

Glancing up at the inflated bag, Jessie realized for the first time that the balloon looked much larger than it really was, and the wicker basket below it looked much smaller than it had when she'd seen it the day before. Ki walked up and stopped beside Jessie and Sanders.

"You're sure you don't want to change your mind and let me be the first to go up?" he asked Jessie.

Jessie shook her head and replied, "I'm sure, Ki. Let's just stick to the plans we made last night and go ahead."

"There's really nothing to worry about," Sanders said. "I don't plan to stay up more than a quarter of an hour or so, just long enough to let Miss Starbuck see that the ideas I've been talking about are practical and not some crazy pipe dream."

"Then you'll take me up after you and Jessie come back to the ground?" Ki asked.

"Just as we agreed to do last night," Sanders nodded. "The wind's very light. The ground wind will carry us east as we gain altitude, and before we've gone too far I'll light the burner and go as high as I need to pick up a cross-current in the upper air. That'll bring us back, and I'll come down as close to the house as I can."

"You sound very positive about being able to maneuver," Ki said.

"Oh, I am." Sanders nodded. "But you'll see for yourself after Jessie and I get in the air." He added, "I'm going to have Nora handle the balloon for your flight. Just to ease your mind, I'll tell you that she's as competent to make an ascension as I am. Her father taught her, and he was one of

26

the finest aeronauts in the country before that accident he had crippled him."

"Crippled?" Jessie asked. "A balloon accident?"

Sanders shook his head. "No, Miss Starbuck. Tim lost his left leg in a train wreck. During all the years he made balloon ascensions he never got so much as a scratch."

"He handles himself very well," Ki said. "I haven't seen him limping."

"Oh, he gets around easily on his artificial leg, but he has trouble getting in and out of a balloon basket. And I couldn't ask for a better crew on the ground than him and Nora."

"I suppose that makes me feel better." Jessie smiled. "But if the—" She stopped short as O'Brien called to Sanders.

"Everything's ready, Ted. You can take it up whenever you've a mind to."

Looking at Jessie, Sanders said, "There's no use waiting around, then. Come along, I'll help you into the basket."

Jessie didn't refuse Sanders' offer to help her, but surprised the aeronaut by grasping the basket's rim and vaulting over it in a single lithe, effortless movement. He blinked but said nothing, then climbed in himself. With both of them in the basket it seemed crowded. Movement in the boxlike basket was limited by a huge coil of rope that occupied most of the bottom, and in the center of the coil there was a metal, bucketlike contrivance that Jessie did not recognize.

Sanders moved at once to stand in the small triangular area diagonally opposite Jessie's position. He was wearing the same coverall that he'd had on the previous day, and Jessie had donned her usual soft clinging blouse and trimly fitted ranch jeans. She'd left her broad-brimmed hat behind, and had tied a bandanna around her head to keep her

27

hair from blowing. Sanders took the leather hood he'd worn the day before from a pocket and held it out to Jessie. She took the hood with its attached goggles and looked questioningly at the aeronaut.

"If we catch a brisk wind when we start going up, your eyes might begin watering," he explained. "If they do, put on the hood."

"Won't you need it?"

"I'm used to the upper air, Miss Starbuck. If the wind aloft gets sharp enough to bother my eyes, I might ask you to give it back to me, but it looks as though we're going to have a smooth ascension."

"Then I won't put this on until I need it," Jessie said. "And since we're going to be crowded together in this little basket for a while, I think it's about time for us to do away with formalities like 'Miss.' Why don't you just call me Jessie?"

"I'll be delighted to. Now, if you're ready—"

"As ready as I'll ever be."

"There's no use wasting time, then." Raising his voice, he called, "We're ready to go up, Tim. Are you going to handle the mooring gear, or will Nora?"

"Nora can do it as well as I can," O'Brien replied. "I'll take care of the pipe."

Pulling on a pair of thick gloves, he pulled the stovepipe free from the hood and held it level while he made his way along it until he'd reached its center. Then he lifted the pipe as a unit, freed it from the basket, and lowered it to the ground. Meanwhile, Nora had reached the side of the balloon.

In spite of her self-assurances that she was in good hands, Jessie's muscles tensed and she tightened her grip on the rim of the basket as Nora bent over the rope that moored the balloon and held it on the ground.

"Now?" Nora asked Sanders.

"Any time," he answered.

"You're free, then," she said, at the same time pulling the slipknot that secured the mooring rope.

To her surprise, Jessie felt no sense of motion. She had been watching Sanders, who was now standing near the center of the basket with his feet spread apart, and saw that he was swaying gently. Then she looked past him and had the sensation that the Circle Star's big main house was sinking and shrinking at the same time. Looking at the bunkhouse and cookshack, she saw that they were also dwindling in size and falling away from her. Only then did the reality sink home that the balloon was actually rising as it moved slowly away from the ranch buildings.

"We—we're going up!" she exclaimed.

"Of course," Sanders said calmly. "That's what we're supposed to do, isn't it?"

"Yes, but I hadn't expected it to be so—well, so smooth and easy."

"Very few people do. It's a sensation that I had a little trouble getting used to myself, when I first began ascending."

As the balloon swept steadily upward, Jessie began staring in amazement at the panorama she was seeing for the first time. On all sides the prairie stretched in an unfamiliar vista. The ground directly below no longer seemed to be level, but looked as though it were slanting upward in all directions from the balloon, and Jessie felt for a moment that she was gazing at the center of a shallow saucer with the horizon forming its rim.

Stock ponds that looked almost colorless when seen on the ground now showed as dots of deep blue. The range that from horseback seemed covered only thinly with grass now glowed green. Barbed wire fences, virtually invisible from a distance at ground level, showed as sharp black lines against the green grasses. The few thickets on the Circle Star range made irregular brownish-green blotches and appeared to be much larger than they were in reality. The main house and the big barn of the Circle Star stood out in bold relief near the center of the vast spread.

"Things are really different when you look at them from up here," Jessie told Sanders.

"A different perspective changes everything," he agreed. "It takes a little while to get used to it, but once you do, everything makes sense."

"How high up are we now?" Jessie asked.

"About eight hundred feet. You won't get a really good look at the area until we lift a bit higher. There's not much wind today, so our drift's going to be very slow. When we get a bit higher, in the upper air currents, we might toss around some, so if I tell you to hold on, just grab the rim of the basket."

Jessie studied the basket for the first time. It was square in shape, its sides coming up almost to her breast, and to her companion's waist. The interwoven lengths of wicker strands of which it was made were the diameter of her fingers, and around its top edge the strands were woven without spaces to form a firm rim. Though it had seemed flimsy at first, the basket now felt quite sturdy and stable. She'd lost the mild uneasiness she'd had when the balloon started skyward, the sensation of being suspended without a safe support, of having nothing solid underfoot.

"You're getting used to it, I see," Sanders commented.

"How did you know?"

"Don't forget, Jessie, I've made several hundred ascensions since I started ballooning. On most of them lately, I've had at least one passenger who was going up for the first time."

"I'll admit I was a little bit nervous." Jessie smiled. "I don't feel nervous at all now, though."

"Good. Now, if you need any help in identifying ground landmarks, just tell me and I'll try to get you oriented."

Jessie hadn't been looking at the ground while she studied the basket. She shifted her eyes now and gasped with surprise at the expanding panorama below.

"Why, I can see Brad Close's place now!" Pointing, she went on, "That's the Box B main house right over there! And some of Brad's hands are standing in front of the bunkhouse, but I can't recognize any of them from such a distance."

"If you'll look in the other direction, you can see the ranch where I landed," Sanders said. "And your own buildings are still in sight, too."

After she'd studied the ground for a few minutes more, Jessie turned to Sanders and said, "I can understand now why you think a balloon would be useful to a ranch. I can see almost all of the Circle Star from up here: cattle, fences, water holes, my hands riding fences—just everything!"

"You'll get an even better view when we go higher," the aeronaut promised. "I'm going to shoot some more hot air into the bag. We'll go up and see if we can't pick up a wind current that'll take us back to where I want to land."

Sanders bent over the bucketlike device that occupied the center of the basket. Removing the lid that covered the top, he reached inside and took out a bottle of water.

"This is my own invention," he explained as he pulled the cork from the bottle. "There's a pan of calcium chloride in the bottom of this cylinder, and when I pour the water on it, it'll start getting hot." He emptied the water down the cylinder, and went on, "I had a tinsmith make up this telescoping tube to carry the heated air up to the bag." He

31

tugged at the rim of the metal cylinder and two more sections slid upward. A wisp of smoky vapor was already emerging from the cylinder as he guided the top into the balloon's dangling vent. "In a few minutes we'll start rising."

At first Jessie wasn't aware of the balloon's rise. Sanders was watching the ground, and nodded with satisfaction as the minutes passed. The big bag began twirling gently, and Jessie's stomach muscles tightened as it swayed. She glanced at the ground and found that the vista she'd been viewing was slowly expanding. The rim of the horizon was widening, objects on the ground growing smaller. The balloon bag tilted a bit, the basket swayed gently, and after a moment Sanders pointed down.

"Watch the ground now," he said. "You'll see that we're going in almost the opposite direction from the way we were moving a few minutes ago. That means we've picked up the upper air current, and we're heading back toward your ranch house again."

After she'd studied the terrain below for several more minutes, Jessie found that she could tell the difference in their direction. The balloon was no longer rising now. The cluster of Circle Star buildings passed below them, and when Sanders made no move Jessie looked at him and frowned.

"I thought we were going to land now," she said.

"We are. I've got to get beyond our landing point, though, because as we go down we'll be in the atmospheric layer where the wind's blowing toward the east."

When they'd gone well beyond the cluster of Circle Star buildings, Sanders busied himself again with the telescoping cylinder, restoring it to its original form. Then he grasped a rope that dangled from the top of the bag and tugged on it. The balloon began to descend slowly. Instinctively, Jessie's hands sought the rim of the basket and grasped it firmly.

"Don't worry," the aeronaut assured her. "I'm just venting some of the hot air, letting it out of the bag. It'll make us descend faster, but don't be alarmed.

"Will we hit very hard when we land?" Jessie asked.

"We won't really land, Jessie. That is, we won't touch ground. But we'll go down just as gently as we lifted off. We'll pick up the ground air current in a few minutes, so don't worry if we sway a little bit when we first get into it."

"Even though everything you've told me has been right so far, I'm still having trouble getting used to the sensation of being up in the air," she replied. "It takes a while to do that, doesn't it?"

"It's easier for some people than others, Jessie. You've been a remarkable passenger, though. I've even had to threaten a few people I've taken up before they'd calm down."

By the time the balloon was a half-mile from the Circle Star headquarters, they were less than a hundred feet above the ground and still descending. Jessie saw the aeronaut's wagon pull away and start toward them, with Ki riding beside it on his horse.

"As soon as they get close enough, I'll let us down faster, so don't worry if you think the ground's coming up to meet us too suddenly," Sanders warned.

"Are you telling me that you can't slow down if you find you're dropping too fast?"

"Oh, no. It just takes a little time to slow a balloon down when it's descending. Luckily, the wind's not too brisk. We shouldn't have any problems."

"Well, that makes me feel better." Jessie smiled. "For a minute I got the same feeling I've had on a runaway horse."

She looked over the side of the basket at the ground. It seemed to be rushing up to meet them. The wagon carrying Tim and Nora O'Brien was still almost a quarter of a mile away, but the balloon was moving toward them, so the distance was closing rapidly. Ki, keeping his horse well away from the wagon, was riding parallel to the course the vehicle was following.

"Another few minutes and we'll be down," Ted said.

He was fishing the end of the rope out of its coil. Jessie watched as he fastened it to a sturdy shackle fixed to the basket rail and pulled still more rope free from the coil on the bottom of the basket. He lifted the freed rope and held it suspended over one side of the basket.

By now the ground seemed very close. Jessie glanced at the wagon and saw that Tim was wheeling it in a wide arc to set it rolling in the same direction the balloon was moving. The ground was only twenty or thirty feet below the basket when Sanders dropped the rope over the side. It streamed behind the basket as it fell and Tim changed the wagon's course, chasing the rope as it hit the ground and trailed snakelike along it.

"Hold tight," Sanders cautioned Jessie. "The basket's going to tilt a bit when the slack goes out of the rope."

Locking her hands over the basket's rim as tightly as her teeth were already clenched, Jessie waited for the rope to grow taut. It lost its slack within a few moments. The basket shook and began to tilt, but Sanders stepped along its slanting floor to the edge and leaned out, and the floor returned to an almost even keel. At the same time the aeronaut began tugging on the rope that released hot air from the balloon's vent on top of the bag. They began to drop

34

more rapidly, the basket swaying with the tugging of the rope.

As the balloon descended the speed of its drop increased. The wagon was directly behind them now. Jessie saw it stop and watched as Tim O'Brien levered himself into its bed. He stretched out, his feet braced against the tailgate. Suddenly Jessie remembered that he had only one leg, and wondered if the artificial leg would be able to bear the strain it must be taking.

She dismissed the thought as foolish, for the balloon was already responding to the tug of the taut rope. It was dropping gently, the basket tilting again as the strain on the rope increased. She kept her grip on the basket's rim, looking with fascination at the ground as it seemed to rise to meet them.

Jessie saw Nora leap from the wagon seat and run to join her father in pulling on the rope. Ki swung off his horse and hurried to add his weight to the rope as well. The bottom of the basket was only a few feet above the ground now, the bag of the balloon leaning away from the wagon. It straightened up slowly, but the basket was slower in responding to the rope's restraint. Then gradually it lost its slant and grew level. Jessie released the sigh of relief she'd been holding, and looked across the basket at Ted Sanders.

"Coming to earth wasn't as bad as I'd thought it would be," she told him.

"Would you go up again?" he asked.

"Of course I would! But right now I'm anxious to let Ki take my place and then see how he feels after his first flight." She turned to lean over the rim of the basket and call, "Come on, Ki! You're about to have an experience you'll never forget!"

Chapter 4

"You don't seem to be a bit nervous for somebody who's going up in the air for the first time," Nora O'Brien told Ki.

She gazed at him curiously across the balloon's swaying basket while the big bag above them was still lifting them into the air. A bit earlier in the day, when she and her father and Ki had been following the balloon across the Circle Star range during Jessie's trip aloft, Ki had noticed the same tiny crease that appeared now between Nora's eyes while she was studying him.

"I'm sure you've heard that we Orientals are never supposed to let our feelings show in our face," he said lightly.

"Are you telling me it's true you don't show anything, then, about the way you feel?"

"No. It's like your Irish legends of the little people."

"Well, if there's anything you want to ask me—" Nora stopped in midsentence, her voice and uplifted eyebrows finishing her question.

"Thanks. I'll probably have a lot of questions later on. Right now, all I want to do for a few minutes is to look and get used to the feeling of being above the ground," Ki replied.

They were still gaining altitude, for Nora's father had

released the mooring rope only a few moments earlier. Ki was experiencing much the same feelings that had come to Jessie at the sight of familiar surroundings viewed from a new perspective. He watched the Circle Star buildings shrinking with the balloon's steady rise, noticed how the sweep of the horizon was increasing, and was now beginning to pick out details of the range—landmarks such as fences and stock ponds and thickets.

With a nod, Nora also turned her attention to the ground, and Ki took the opportunity to study her for a moment while her eyes were away from him.

Ki judged her to be in her middle twenties, a sturdily built woman with square shoulders and wide hips. Her first preparation for taking the balloon aloft had been to step into a pair of farmer-type bib overalls, and the bib did not conceal but rather emphasized the rounded fullness of her breasts. Nora's face was just a bit too broad, but this failed to detract from the effect of her red-bronze hair and deep-blue eyes above high cheekbones, her generous lips and rounded chin.

"You'll be able to see a lot more as we go higher," she told Ki. She took her eyes off the Circle Star range and began searching the horizon, pointing to the east. "Ted said he started looking for a crosswind as soon as he could see the ranch that's off yonder."

"Brad Close's Box B," Ki said.

"Oh, yes." Nora nodded. "We'll watch for it, then, and when we see it I'll start putting more hot air into the bag."

"You act as though this is something you do every day," Ki commented. Then he went on quickly, "But I guess it is, isn't it? I can't get used to the idea, myself."

"Balloons are quite new to you? I thought the Japanese had experimented with them." Nora frowned and added, "Or is it the Chinese I'm thinking about?"

37

"I'm sure both my people and the Chinese also have flown balloons. There's very little we haven't tried," Ki told her. "But in the Far East we mainly fly kites. Not just as toys, either. In Japan and China and Korea kites are taken very seriously. More than a hundred years ago we Orientals were making kites big enough to carry a man aloft."

"Now, that's something I didn't know," Nora said. "But as far as that goes, I'm afraid I don't know much about the history of balloons, either."

"That's odd." Ki frowned. "I remember Ted telling Jessie and me that your father was a famous balloonist before he lost his leg in an accident."

"So he was, but Da's a practical man, Ki. He's very good with balloons, but he's never been a scholar."

"I see." Ki nodded. Before they could pick up the conversation again, he glanced over the rim of the basket and said, "I can see Brad Close's place now. Didn't you say that's where Ted told you to start going higher?"

"Yes." Nora looked at the Box B buildings on the ground ahead of them. "I'll start the heater. It'll take a while for us to go up. If we're lucky the same crosswind Ted used will still be blowing, and it'll take us back to the Circle Star."

"Suppose we're not lucky?" Ki asked. "What will we do if we don't find the crosswind?"

"Keep going higher until we do," Nora replied, looking at him over her shoulder as she began pouring water into the metal container that held the calcium chloride. "When you're aloft, you can always find a crosscurrent in the upper air. All you have to do is go high enough."

"It sounds very simple, the way you explain it."

"Oh, it's not really all that cut-and-dried, Ki. But I've learned enough about ballooning to handle almost anything we're likely to run into during a short ascension like this one."

Ki glanced at the ground again and saw that the buildings of the Box B were changing form. They seemed to be shrinking very slowly. He looked beyond them and found that the line of the horizon seemed much farther away. Then he realized that the changes he was noticing were due to the balloon's speedier rise.

"Tell me if I'm wrong, Nora," he said, "but aren't we rising faster now than we did when we left the ground?"

"Quite a bit," she confirmed. "I've had it happen before, though. Ted told me that there are what he calls pockets in the upper air. The way he explained it, they're something like the bubbles in water."

"And we're in one now?"

"I'm sure we are."

"How big are these pockets?"

"I haven't any idea, Ki, and I don't think anybody else has. There still aren't any rules about them."

By this time the balloon was going up very swiftly indeed. Ki glanced at the ground and saw the objects on it shrinking a great deal faster than when they'd first ascended.

"How high are we now?" he asked Nora.

"I'd guess about three thousand feet."

"More than half a mile, and still going up?"

Nora nodded. "We must be in an unusually big air pocket. I'd better stop adding hot air. We're going up a lot faster than I'd expected we would." Dropping to one knee, she put the close-fitting lid on the metal container holding the calcium chloride. Looking over her shoulder at Ki, she went on, "And we're likely to be—"

Before she could finish her explanation, the big bag above them seemed to lean to one side, then the leaning movement became a sudden sharp jump. The basket began swaying and, without warning, tilted sharply as the bag suddenly swirled in a three-quarter turn. The ropes that held the basket suspended twisted as the basket began gyrating crazily, its weight causing it to respond belatedly to the bag's unexpected movement.

Nora was still half-kneeling above the chemical container, and the basket's sudden tilting swirl caught her off-balance and tossed her sidewise. Ki released his grip on the basket's rim and dived for her, trying to keep her from falling. He managed to get his arms around her and ease her fall, and Nora locked her hands around his upper arm, but his balance was too precarious to be maintained. Nora's weight pulled him down with her to the bottom of the swaying, tossing basket. They landed and slid until they reached the basket's side, where they lay sprawled in a curled tangle of arms and legs.

Above them the balloon's bag was righting itself slowly, but the basket still swayed. For a moment or two it came to a total stop, then it started swaying again, rotating as the twisted ropes that supported it began to straighten out.

Nora was lying at an angle to the basket's bottom, partly on her side, partly on her back. One thigh was below Ki's hips, the other between his legs. She tried to shift her position, but Ki's weight kept her pinned down, while their tangle of arms and legs prevented either of them from moving freely.

"We'd better just lie still until the basket stops," she told Ki, gazing above him at the still-twisting ropes that ran from the basket's corners to the meshlike network of smaller ropes that enclosed the bag. "We might run into another pocket of dead air as we go higher."

"I can stand it if you can," Ki replied. "You must be a lot more uncomfortable than I am."

"I don't mind it," she said quickly. "This isn't the first time I've been pinned under—" Realizing belatedly what her unthinking admission implied, she stopped short but lay gazing up into Ki's face without making any effort to move.

Her tongue-slip surprised Ki almost as much as it did Nora herself. He stared down into her eyes and saw them crinkling at the corners as a mischievous grin spread across her face. Before he could think of a suitable reply, she spoke again.

"Don't look so surprised, Ki," she went on. "You must've realized by now that I'm not some prissy little missy that was brought up in a front parlor by a doting family."

"If I hadn't realized it before, I do now," Ki replied. "I was just thinking that this is an unusual place for me to be in this position with a pretty woman, but I couldn't think of a way to say anything without shocking you."

"I'm practically shockproof," Nora confessed, her smile growing wider. She glanced above Ki's shoulder at the bag of the balloon and saw that it was moving slowly to its usual upright position, then went on, "And I like for unexpected things to happen to me, as long as they're pleasant. But don't you think we'd be a little bit cramped in this basket?"

"I'm sure we could manage something that wouldn't be too uncomfortable," Ki told her. He'd been isolated on the Circle Star for almost three months, and Nora's sudden suggestion had reminded him how long he'd been away from women. "If you're really serious about going on with what we seem to have started accidentally."

"It'd be something new," she said. "A time or two, I've thought about how private it would be with a man, up in the air this way, but you're the first one I've run into who

41

seems to share my thoughts."

This time, Ki consciously kept his face from reflecting his surprise. He asked her, "You really are serious, then?"

"Give me a minute or so to be sure we're going into the crosswind we've been looking for, and we'll see what we can work out."

A bit reluctantly, Ki got to his feet. Nora followed him, and looked over the rim of the basket to study the ground. Ki looked below, too. They'd passed over the Box B headquarters during their drift toward the east, before the balloon had begun rising. Now Brad Close's house and the other ranch buildings were almost directly below them again. Nora straightened up with an exhalation of relief.

"We're moving back toward the Circle Star," she said. "But this upper air current's more sluggish than the one we were in lower to the ground. We'll have plenty of time, if you're still in the mood."

"Nothing's happened to change my mind."

"I was sure you wouldn't, but thought I'd better ask." A challenge in her eyes as well as her voice. Nora said, "Try me, if you still have any doubts."

Ki stepped closer to her and took her in his arms. Nora pressed herself to him as he sought her mouth, and met his tongue when he thrust it forward between their clinging lips. While they prolonged their kiss, her hand moved to his crotch and as her fingers moved in eager question, stroking, and squeezing, Ki quickly felt himself grow erect.

As Nora's busy fingers continued to caress him, Ki broke their kiss and gently slid his lips to her throat. He ran his fingertips ahead of his lips, found the buttons at the back of her low-cut blouse, and loosed those at the top. Nora shrugged her shoulders to aid him in slipping aside the straps that supported the overalls. With a quick twist of

42

her shoulders she let both overalls and blouse slide to her waist.

Ki followed their fall with his lips. Brushing them softly over the silk-soft warmth of Nora's rosy-budded tips, he took them into his mouth one after the other. As his tongue-tip caressed them gently, Nora began to quiver. The first gentle undulations of her body grew into continuing shudders, and after Ki had been at his caresses for a few minutes she twisted herself free and pushed her hands against his chest to break their embrace. Ki raised his head and looked at her questioningly.

He asked, "Is this as far—"

"Of course not!" she broke in impatiently. "I wasn't just leading you on!"

While she spoke, Nora twisted her hips to let the overalls slip to the floor of the basket. She pulled up her skirt and untied the drawstring of her knee-length pantalettes, and when they slipped down her legs to fall in a heap on the overalls she levered her feet out of her low-heeled pumps and stepped away from the crumpled heap of overalls.

"I think this is as much undressing as I'd better do," Nora told him as she pushed the little heap of clothing aside with one bare foot. "Not that there's anyone up here to watch us, but if the current should suddenly speed up, they'd be able to see us from the ground. I try to keep my personal life to myself."

Nora's movements had been so swiftly efficient that Ki was still watching her in surprise when she moved away from the little pile of her discarded garments. He quickly pulled the knot of the drawstring that supported his loose trousers, his eyes on Nora's swaying breasts and the glow of her light-bronze pubic fleece. The trousers fell to his ankles and he stepped free.

Nora's eyes went at once to Ki's jutting erection and her hands instantly followed her eyes. She squeezed him gently, then looked up at the round symmetrical bulges of his biceps and forearms. Her hands closed tighter around his erection as she said, "You're stronger than I realized, Ki. Lift me up! I want to feel this in me, not just look at it!"

Ki lifted her effortlessly. Nora opened her thighs as he brought her up, and she lifted her legs to wrap them around Ki's hips. She locked her ankles and pulled herself slowly toward him, sighing as he went into her.

For a moment Nora did not move except to clasp her hands behind Ki's neck. She held on with her head thrown back and her eyes closed, her full lips parted in an ecstatic smile. Ki thrust, and she gasped as he completed his penetration. Then she began rolling her hips from side to side while Ki stroked with short quick jabs that brought groans of delight from her lips.

"Oh, yes!" she moaned, her head resting on Ki's shoulder, her lips brushing his ear. "But go slower for a little while now, Ki. I want to enjoy this for a long time!"

Ki shifted his thrusting to a slower, steadier tempo. Nora pulled herself closer, until her breasts pressed his chest, and she twisted her shoulders from side to side to rub their tips across his smooth flesh. The added sensation brought her new sighs of pleasure, and Ki bent his head forward to find her lips with his. They swayed in unison, tongues entwined, until she suddenly began trembling.

"I can't wait any longer!" she gasped as she broke their kiss. "I want to hold on, but—oh! Oh!"

Ki pulled Nora closer to him, holding her tightly, and kept thrusting slowly until her quivering body warned him that she was nearing her climax. Then he braced his elbows and held her suspended by her armpits while he lengthened his strokes and began pounding faster.

44

Nora's throaty gasps turned into short ecstatic screams. Ki speeded up, driving with long lusty lunges until Nora's frantic cries became deep moans of gratification. He clasped her to his chest and held her while the trembling that had seized her faded and she sagged limp and motionless in his muscular arms.

Several minutes ticked past before Nora's ragged breathing became regular. She stirred, raised her head and leaned away from him, looking into his face with a puzzled frown. Her voice showing her perplexity, she asked, "You didn't—"

Shaking his head, Ki broke in, "I thought you might like to go on a while longer."

"You must've known I would." She smiled. "I'm really greedy about some things, Ki, and this is one of them. But aren't you tired of holding me up?"

"No. You're not that heavy."

"Start again whenever you're ready, then."

Holding Nora suspended in front of him, Ki began thrusting slowly and rhythmically again. Nora's eyes closed after a moment or two and she started twisting her hips in a rolling rhythm that matched his measured stroking.

Her response was quicker this time, and equally as enthusiastic. Only a few minutes passed before her gasping and the spasmodic jerking of her hips told Ki that she was reaching another climax. He was more than ready to join her by now, and speeded up his deep thrusts.

"Hurry, Ki!" she urged. "I can't wait any longer!"

"Neither can I," Ki gasped.

He lunged like a trip-hammer now while Nora clung to him, her hips gyrating frantically, her head thrown back, eyes squeezed shut, while Ki pounded into her with a final finishing stroke, pulled her to him, and held fast while their bodies shuddered into the final seconds of total gratification. Bracing his feet, Ki held Nora's soft, warm body pressed to his until she stirred again and sighed.

"I think you'd better let go of me," she said. "Not that I want you to, but you must be really tired by now."

"I could use a rest," Ki admitted.

He released her and Nora dropped to her feet. She stood looking into his eyes for a moment, then leaned forward and kissed him quickly. Then she turned away, glanced around, and gasped with surprise.

Lost in their sensations, neither Ki nor Nora had given any thought to their position. Ahead of the balloon and almost level with the basket a bank of clouds was forming fast, with the unpredictable, swift change of Texas weather. Dark-gray wisps were streaming from the upper atmosphere to join the roiling line that had already taken shape and was now stretching levelly for several miles on both sides of the balloon.

"We've got to drop fast," Nora said, hurrying to get her clothing on again. "We'll get wet when we go down, but if we don't get below that cloudbank, we might be in real trouble."

Ki peered over the rim of the basket and pointed at the ground ahead. "We're almost over the Circle Star buildings," she said. "Is it too risky to get closer to them before we go down?"

"We'll have to drop faster than I like to," she told him. "But if we're lucky, we can just about make it. Grab the basket and hold on."

Ki locked his hands on the basket rim as Nora reached for the cord that dangled from the balloon's spout. She pulled it, opening the panel of fabric in the top of the bag that allowed the hot air to gush out. The basket began rocking as they started to descend. A vagrant air current caught the bag as it went lower and twirled the basket, setting it rocking harder.

Nora braced her feet a bit wider and clung to the exhaust cord to steady herself. Ki reached one hand to her and she grasped it. The balloon was twirling faster now, but it was going down fast. Ahead, Ki could see the sheen of raindrops falling from the clouds.

A wind-gust caught the big bag, making it heel sharply as it entered the falling rain. The ropes that held the basket to the balloon jerked and started the basket bouncing. Ki fought to hold his grip on the rim as raindrops began pelting them.

A second, harder gust hit them before they'd recovered from the first. It tilted the basket until its bottom was almost straight up and down, and Ki felt his hand slipping on the wet wicker of the basket rim.

Nora was clinging to his other hand, her feet sliding on the rain-slickened bottom of the basket as she fought to keep her balance. The rain was pelting them like tiny needles now, and when a fresh gust of wind jarred the craft, Nora lost the struggle to stay on her feet. The soles of her shoes slid across the slanting bottom of the basket and she swung over empty space, clinging to Ki's hand while he fought to keep his grip on the slick wicker rail.

Chapter 5

"Hold tight, Ki!" Nora urged.

"I'm doing the best I can," Ki replied. "But this rain's made everything so slick—" He broke off as the basket began twirling slowly.

Nora was struggling to reach Ki's wrist with her free hand, but the rotation of the basket had set her to swaying. After a few moments of frantic clawing she managed to grasp his wrist and, with both hands clinging to him, she was at last able to stop her twisting. Without the impetus given it by Nora's movements, the basket slowly stopped turning. Both Nora and Ki breathed more easily then, and as the williwawing gusts passed the bag righted itself and the basket dropped back to its normal position.

Planting her feet on the bottom of the basket, Nora let go of Ki's hand and wrist. He was still in the awkward posture into which the balloon's gyrations had tossed him, gripping the rim with one hand, half-standing, half-sprawled on one side of the basket. With a quick, light move Ki regained his feet.

"That was a little bit close," he said.

"Too close for comfort," Nora said. Her voice was calm, as though their recent close shave was a commonplace occurrence. "We're lucky that squall didn't hit us a few minutes earlier."

"That could have been embarrassing." Ki smiled.

"You know without me telling you how grateful I am that you saved me," Nora went on, speaking quickly as though she wanted to dismiss the incident. Looking toward the ground she motioned toward the Circle Star's buildings, which the sudden push of wind had put behind them. "But we're all right now."

Ki looked back in the direction of Nora's gesture. The balloon's tender-wagon was moving away from the corral, and Jessie was riding beside it on Sun, a saddled horse trailing her on a lead-rope. The balloon had lost altitude during the passing of the wind. He frowned as he tried to gauge their height with his eyes.

"Aren't we about three hundred feet high?" he asked Nora.

"Perhaps a little less," she said. "We lost a lot of altitude when that wind hit us. I'll start taking us down now. By the time we're low enough to land, Da and Ted and Jessie will be almost directly under us."

Above them the sky was now clear, the upper air currents carrying away the line of gray clouds that had seemed so menacing while the balloon was at their edge. When Ki looked down he could see small puffs of dust thrown up by the horses' hooves. The balloon kept dropping slowly but steadily, and the party on the ground was only a short distance away.

"What can I do to help when we're landing?" Ki asked.

"Nothing. You saw how simple it was when you were watching Ted bring the bag down after he took Jessie up. He'll stop the wagon downwind and a little bit ahead of us. All I have to do is toss out the rope for him to grab as we pass over. Then I'll pull the vent open wider while he and Da haul in, and we'll settle down like a feather."

"It sounds easy, the way you put it."

49

"It is easy," Nora told him as she bent to free the coil of rope from the cord ties that held it in place. She carried it to one side of the basket and, when Ki moved toward her, waved him away. "Stand on the side opposite me," she said. "That's to distribute our weight evenly so we won't tilt as we land."

"One basket-tilt a day is my limit." Ki smiled. "The one we had a while ago was all I needed."

"It could've been serious," Nora agreed. "But we can talk about that later on." Her eyes questioning, she added, "I hope there will be a later on for us."

"Don't worry about that," he assured her. "And we'll have more time and be more comfortable. You're going to stay here at the Circle Star for a while, aren't you?"

"I suppose so. At least until Jessie decides whether or not she'll back Ted in trying out some of his ideas."

"Jessie's not afraid to try new things," Ki said. "She's just like her father was."

"Was? He's dead, then?"

Ki nodded. "He was murdered here on the Circle Star by a bunch of hired assassins who were sent by a—"

Ki hesitated momentarily, trying to think of a way to condense the story of the defunct cartel into as few words as possible. He knew that someone like Nora, to whom the world of big business was totally strange, would have trouble understanding how a lust for money and power could turn men into monsters such as the cartel bosses had been. In the end, he compromised.

"By some of his business enemies," he finished.

"And he left the ranch to Jessie?"

"Yes. Not only the ranch, of course, but all his other businesses as well. The Circle Star's just one of the properties she inherited from Alex."

"But where do you fit into things, Ki?" Nora frowned.

"It isn't any of my business, of course, but I'm curious. If Jessie inherited everything from her father, where do you fit in?"

"That's too long a story to go into now," Ki broke in. He motioned toward the wagon, which by this time was a very short distance from the balloon and closing fast. "I wouldn't even have time to begin before we land."

Nora glanced down. The balloon was little more than twenty feet above the ground now, drifting slowly toward the approaching wagon, and Tim O'Brien was sawing at the reins to turn the horse. Jessie had already pulled Sun to a halt at a distance from the vehicle and was sitting in the saddle, her face turned up, watching the balloon's approach.

Ted pushed himself over the back of the seat into the wagonbed and waved as the light ground wind took the balloon ever closer. Nora lifted the coiled rope over the basket rim and let it fall. Paying out from the coil, the rope streamed out behind the drifting balloon. Tim reined the wagon horse to bring the belly of the rope into Ted's reach, and as he grabbed it and snubbed it around his hips the rope slowly straightened out.

Ki was conscious of only a slight tilting of the basket as the rope grew taut. Above him, the bag of the balloon swayed as it began leaning away, and he felt the basket shudder slightly under his feet.

Then the wagon came to a halt. Tim O'Brien stepped over the back of the seat into the bed of the wagon and gave Ted a hand with the rope. The bag of the balloon was still tilted a bit, but as the basket grated against the wagonbed and came to a halt, the bag slowly straightened up, its sides now wrinkling and beginning to sag. Looking at Nora, Ki gestured to her to get out of the basket, but she shook her head.

"Passengers get out first," she said. "I've still got a few little things to do, anyhow."

Ignoring the hand that Tim O'Brien extended, Ki vaulted over the side of the basket and landed lightly in the wagonbed.

"Well?" Ted asked. "How did you like it?"

"Very much," Ki said.

"From here on the ground, it looked like you ran into a patch of roiled air," Ted went on. "How bad was it?"

"Not bad at all," Ki replied. "Nora got us out of it right away. She's a very good aeronaut, Ted."

"She'd better be," Tim O'Brien put in as he looked up from the snubbed rope he'd been examining. "I taught her meself, and grown woman or not, I'd still blister her bottom if she put me to shame by making a mistake."

"Now, Da, you shouldn't talk like I'm still a little girl in a pinafore!" Nora protested playfully. "And you mustn't think I'd let you down, either."

"I'm not, lass," Tim replied. "I was watching when you ran into them rain clouds, and I was right proud of the way you handled the bag."

"Oh, that bit of weather we ran into wasn't really bad." She shrugged. "Just a few drops of rain and a little breeze. I've handled a lot worse, and you know it."

Before Tim could answer, Jessie rode up and reined in beside the wagon.

"Did you enjoy going up as much as I did?" she asked Ki.

"I'm sure I did," Ki said. "At least, I'm ready to go up again, if there's any chance of it."

"There might be a better chance than you think," she told him. "After talking with Ted, and taking that flight in the balloon myself, I've had an idea."

"It has something to do with the balloon, I hope," Ted broke in, looking up from the basket.

"Yes, it does." Jessie nodded. "But it's going to take you a while to finish your work here, and I'd like to talk with Ki about it first." She turned to Ki and went on, "If you're ready to go now, we can talk things over while we're riding back to the house, then go over it with Ted when he gets there."

"Whatever you say," Ki replied. He took the reins of the horse Jessie had been leading and swung into the saddle. With a wave to Ted and the others, he turned the animal and rode beside Jessie as they started toward the Circle Star's headquarters.

"Now that you've been up, do you feel the way I do about the balloon, Ki?" Jessie asked after they'd put a little distance between themselves and the wagon.

"It doesn't bother me to be up in the air, if that's what you mean."

"That's part of it. The rest is how much you can see from up above. I got an entirely fresh view of the Circle Star while I was sailing over it. Did you?"

"I certainly saw things from above that I never noticed when I was riding past them on the ground. Have you ever taken a good look at the eastern line fence between the Circle Star and the Box B?"

"Do you mean there's something wrong with it?"

"Nothing important, but the fence around Brad's nursery pasture doesn't follow the Box B property line. About a mile from the southwestern corner it starts slanting to take in a water hole that's on Circle Star range."

Jessie frowned as she said, "I've never noticed that, Ki, and I've ridden along that line fence—well, I don't know how many times."

53

"Neither had I. And it doesn't make much difference as long as Brad has the Box B. But if he sold the ranch, you might not want the new owner to have even a little piece of property that's yours by right. You might have an argument on your hands."

"Just offhand, I can see my father letting Brad have that hole," Jessie said thoughtfully. "But you're right, Ki. We might not have the same feeling for a new owner that we do for Brad, and you know he's been wanting to retire for quite a while."

"That was the first thing I thought about when I noticed the fence. It struck me that it might be a good idea to float that balloon along all the property-line fences. But from what you said a minute ago, you had the same thought."

"Not exactly. I was thinking about the Silver City mine, and wondering if I could be wrong about Dan Coats stealing silver. The lode just might be petering out, you know. That started me thinking about doing some more prospecting, and I wondered if there could be a way to do it from a balloon."

"Have you asked Ted about the idea?"

"I haven't had a chance to, yet. But I intend to ask him when he gets back to the house. Maybe after supper this evening."

"I've never heard of anybody prospecting from a balloon," Ki said, frowning.

"Neither have I," Jessie agreed, "but there's always somebody who has to try a new idea for the first time."

"Well, it won't cost anything to talk about it," Ki told her. "There might just be some way to work it out."

They rode on in companionable silence, enjoying the luxury of peace, to which they still hadn't gotten quite accustomed. As their horses set their own pace across the richly grassed Circle Star range, Jessie wondered how long it would be before she and Ki adjusted to the fact that the vicious outlaws and hired killers of the cartel no longer posed a threat of constant danger.

From her own experience, Jessie knew that the idea of peace was slow in taking root. There'd been few days when she'd been able to relax fully since the smoke of the final battle against the enemies who had assassinated Alex Starbuck and had become hers in turn had cleared.

Turning to Ki, she said, "We haven't talked about it much, but do you still sleep with one eye open, even though you know the cartel isn't going to attack the Circle Star ever again?"

"It's a hard habit to break," Ki replied soberly. "But now that Ingram Harcourt's dead and most of his hired killers as well, I think we'll get used to the idea that the cartel died with Harcourt."

"And you don't think someone else will come along who'll try to repeat what he almost succeeded in doing?"

"Not any time soon, at least, Jessie. Harcourt had the kind of scheming, merciless mind that only occurs in men once every century or so."

"That's what I keep reminding myself," Jessie confessed. "But somehow I can't keep from reaching for my Colt when I wake up suddenly in the middle of the night, maybe from hearing some strange noise, or maybe just from imagining that I did."

"Be patient," Ki said. "Destroying the cartel became such a part of our lives that it's going to take time to put it out of our minds for good."

"I'm glad I finally asked you," Jessie told him. "Maybe I'll feel better now, knowing I'm not alone in the way I feel."

• • •

In the room that had been her father's favorite and was now Jessie's, she and Ki were sitting with Ted Sanders. The mellow glow of lamplight on the painting of Jessie's dead mother created the illusion that the portrait was a living woman, ready to step from the frame. The picture somehow transmitted its vitality to the matching painting of Alex Starbuck, which now filled the space between the twin windows across the room.

Jessie had gazed at that space many times since Alex's death, and had formed a mental image of the way Alex's picture would look. Somehow, though, she'd been unable to bring herself to place her father's image in the room until his cowardly assassination had been avenged. Soon after the final battle against the cartel, she'd finally commissioned the portrait, and during the short time since it had been put in place the room, with its many mementos of Alex, had taken on a new meaning.

His battered oak desk, the first piece of furniture Alex had bought when he opened the curio shop in San Francisco that had been his original business venture, stood in the place it had always occupied, but it looked somehow different. So did the leather-upholstered armchair that had been his favorite, and still held a faint trace of the fragrance of his cherry-flavored pipe tobacco. This was the chair in which Jessie was now sitting, while Ted Sanders and Ki had made themselves comfortable on the sofa across from her.

Jessie had just finished outlining her idea for using the balloon to float above the area around the Starbuck mine in New Mexico and survey the ground in search of surface formations, like the one above the rich silver mine she and Ki had discovered a few years earlier.

"I won't pretend to know whether it's a good idea or not, Jessie," Ted Sanders said after listening to Jessie's explanation of her idea. "I don't know if anyone's ever thought of using a balloon to survey for minerals before, but I'm sure nobody's ever tried it. If they had, I'd be likely to know about it."

"Whether or not it's been done before doesn't bother me, Ted," she replied. "My father always told me that unless I had enough faith in my ideas to try them myself, nobody else was likely to try them for me."

"Alex Starbuck was a successful man because he had faith in himself," Ki put in before Sanders could speak. "He made a fortune just by using new ideas that came to him, and I know that Jessie has added to her inheritance by taking some new paths she's thought of."

"Just give me your opinion, Ted," Jessie said. "That's all I want right now."

After a moment's thought, Sanders said, "I'm not passing judgment on your ideas, Jessie. I think everything would depend on how much you can tell about what's underground just from looking at the surface, and I don't know all that much about silver mining."

"It won't take you very long to look at the land over two or three of the mines around Silver City," Jessie said. "If the ground above them has some identifying characteristic, all you'd have to do is sail over another area and see if you can find the same pattern being repeated."

"It sounds logical enough." Sanders nodded. "I'm sure willing to give it a try."

"Then all we have left to do is to decide on your fee," Jessie went on. "I'll pay you whatever's fair, of course, and cover the cost of shipping your wagon and equipment."

"You mean we won't have to bounce around in the wagon for a week or so?" Ted smiled. "That's a luxury we don't often have when we travel, and I somehow have the idea that this Silver City place is pretty well off the beaten track."

"It was until a year or so ago," Ki volunteered. "But now the Southern Pacific's built a spur up from Deming. They were working on it the last time Jessie and I went up to look at the mine."

"Yes, it's only a three-day trip now," Jessie added. "But you'll need a baggage car to hold your equipment, so I'll send a man to the depot to order it. Since there'll be a lot of extra room, I think I'll send Sun and a horse for Ki as well. How long will it take you to get ready?"

"Tim and Nora and I are all used to moving around, Jessie," Ted reminded her. "We can leave tomorrow, if you want to. But we'll have to stop somewhere, some good-sized town, where I can buy all the calcium chloride I'll need. I'll want to carry more rope than we usually do, too, and patching materials for the bag. There'll probably be a few other things I'll need, but in a large town I won't have any trouble finding them."

"El Paso will be your best bet," Ki volunteered. "There's a fair amount of mining being done around there, and the town's big enough now to have some wholesale hardware houses."

"That sounds fine," Ted said. "When do we start?"

"As soon as you can get ready," Jessie replied. "It's going to take a few days for me to tie up loose ends, so suppose you start whenever your baggage car gets here. Ki and I will meet you in El Paso and we'll go on together from there."

Chapter 6

"Silver City's grown," Ki," Jessie commented as they topped the last rise in the winding road and saw the town spread below in its little hollow, outlined sharply by the late-morning sun.

"And more than a little bit," Ki agreed.

A short distance behind them Ted Sanders, Nora, and her father were following in the wagon. Ki looked back. Nora caught his eyes, smiled, and winked. Ki nodded imperceptibly.

Since he and Jessie had rejoined the balloonists, he and Nora had been unable to communicate with anything more than their eyes except for a brief moment during the bustle of unloading at the Southern Pacific railhead, which was still more than ten miles from Silver City. During those few seconds they'd managed only to exchange regrets, and Ki took her smile as a promise for the future. Then Jessie spoke again, and Ki returned his attention to her.

"I'm sure it's because the railroad's building a spur into the town," she went on. "And Dan Coats has mentioned in his reports that three more mines have been opened up since we were here last."

Jessie and Ki rode on in silence, looking ahead at the town they were approaching. New cut-stone buildings had replaced most of the hastily erected stores that had dominated the town's main business street at the time of their earlier visit. On both sides of the commercial section new houses dotted the little hollow in which the town lay.

"And I see there's a new livery stable, too," Jessie said, pointing to a sign at the edge of the town's clustered buildings. "I certainly wouldn't want to leave Sun to be cared for by those dreadful men who gave us trouble when we were here before."

"I'm sure that's not the only change we'll find," Ki told her as they reached the level floor of the little basin. "There'll probably be a new restaurant or two where we can get a good meal, and a decent hotel with comfortable beds."

A few minutes more and they were dismounting in front of the livery stable. As usual, Sun drew the attention of all the idlers who frequented the establishment. Jessie had no sooner dismounted than a half-dozen men were clustered around the big palomino. Two men came out of the stable office. One walked up to Sun and began examining him, the other stopped in front of Jessie and Ki. He frowned when he saw Ki's Oriental features, then turned to gaze at Jessie, a questioning look on his face.

"You folks'll be wanting to board your horses, I guess?" he asked, his voice uncertain as he looked from Jessie to Ki.

"Of course," Jessie replied, her voice crisp with authority. "And if you're concerned about your bill, it'll be paid promptly by the Starbuck mine on the other side of town. I'm Jessica Starbuck."

"Ephalet Tittle, ma'am, at your service," the liveryman said, touching the brim of his battered hat. "Sorry I didn't know who you are, but I guess you ain't been here since I opened up my place."

Before Jessie could reply, the man who'd come out of

the office with Tittle turned away from his admiring examination of Sun and stepped up to her.

"I couldn't help overhearing you, Miss Starbuck," he said. "And I hope you'll excuse me for butting in. My name's Will Talley, and I want to thank you for what you did for me."

Jessie looked at him. Talley was a clean-cut, open-faced man who appeared to be about midway into his years of early maturity. He had on a simple business suit, a stockman's hat with a conservative Colorado crease, and plain-toed boots. Jessie was sure that she'd have remembered Talley if she'd ever seen him before.

Hiding her bewilderment, she asked, "Have we met somewhere else, Mr. Talley? I'm afraid I don't recall seeing you when I was here in Silver City before."

"No, ma'am." Talley flipped back his coat lapel to show the badge pinned to his vest and went on, "I'm the town marshal now, but if you hadn't showed up that crooked Tate Nolan who held down the marshal's office the last time you were here, I never would've got the job."

"I certainly don't want you to feel indebted to me for that," Jessie told Talley. "My trouble with Marshal Nolan was a business matter, and I didn't have a thing to do with getting you the job he was holding."

"Just the same, I'm grateful to you," Talley insisted. "Nolan had the town buffaloed. If it hadn't been for you showing him up for the crook he was, he'd still be running things."

"Perhaps so." Jessie nodded. "But I'm sure you got the job on your own merits. Now, if you'll excuse me, I've got to see to the business that I've come here to settle."

"Sure," Talley replied. "But you remember, if I can help you while you're here in Silver City, just let me know."

"Thank you, I will," Jessie replied. Talley touched the

brim of his hat and turned away. She stepped over to Ki, who was talking to the livery's owner, and asked, "Have you arranged things with Mr. Tittle, Ki?"

"It's fairly well settled," Ki told her. "Tim insisted on staying here at the stable, to keep anybody who's curious about the balloon from meddling with it, and Mr. Tittle has a small room that he can use. Ted and Nora want to help unload the gear and check it over, so Tim will bring them into town later. I told them I'd arrange for their rooms at the hotel."

Jessie nodded. "That sounds fine. I think I'd like to look the town over before we go out to the mine to talk to Dan Coats, so let's go ahead and settle in. It's likely that we'll be here for quite a while."

Even before Jessie and Ki reached the center of town it was plain to them that Silver City had indeed changed. The biggest change could not be seen until they turned off Bullard Street into Broadway. Most of the higgledy-piggledy shacks and raw, unpainted buildings that had marked the main thoroughfare on their earlier visit had vanished, and in their place were neatly painted stores and even several imposing brick structures. The character of the residents seemed to have changed also. There were fewer loafers on the streets and more overall-clad miners, and there was also a scattering of women doing family shopping.

"It looks like this might grow up to be a nice town, Ki," Jessie commented. "I think I like the idea of having had a little bit to do with getting the crooks and swindlers cleared out of it. Let's check into that hotel ahead and have a bite of lunch, then we'll go out to the mine and see if my suspicions are correct."

"When we get to the mine, Ki, I want you to keep Coats occupied while I go over his books," Jessie said.

They were riding along the half-remembered road—a bit more than a meandering trail now—that led to the Starbuck silver mine. The afternoon sun was touching the tops of the tall ponderosa pines that stood wide-spaced on each side of the gently slanting slope out of which the road had been gouged, and the low-growing piñon pines that were the only other growth in the semiarid country were already casting pools of shadow on the ground around them.

Nature was already reclaiming the barren areas that had been used by the Indians and early-arriving Spaniards for the crude little one-man smelting furnaces so prominent when Jessie and Ki had first visited the area. Now the only evidence these had ever existed were a few piles of crumbling adobe bricks, and here and there a shallow pit where the ore-bearing soil had been excavated years ago.

"Suppose I ask Coats to show me some places where we can launch the balloon," Ki suggested. "That'll get him out of the office long enough for you to check the books, and I'd imagine it's unusual enough to keep him from being surprised because you don't go along. But won't it take you quite a while to find out how he's hiding the thefts?"

"There are only a few ways for him to falsify production figures, Ki," Jessie said. "And I'm already familiar with most of them. Embezzlers usually follow the same pattern, because bookkeeping systems have to be pretty much the same."

"Then if Coats is really stealing, there'll be evidence of it in his records, even if he tries to hide it."

"Of course." Jessie nodded. "Figures don't lie, and even when liars change them there's always a clue to what really happened if you just look closely enough."

"How long do you think it'll take you to find what you're looking for?" Ki asked.

"I haven't any idea. Just don't say anything to Coats

that might warn him what I'm looking for until I've got some solid evidence I'm right. Just keep him away from the office as long as you can this afternoon, and I'll work as fast as possible."

"This is the craziest idea I've ever heard of!" Daniel Coats exclaimed, reining his horse to a halt. "Finding a silver lode by sailing over the country in a balloon!"

Coats was a bulky man in his middle or later forties. His face showed the effects of years spent in the rough-and-tumble underground battle between miners and nature. In addition to several small scars from wounds that had healed long ago, one of his cheeks and the blurred line of his prominent jawbone were corrugated from the effects of a long-ago explosion in a mineshaft, which had imbedded tiny specks of grit beneath the skin. His hands were pudgy, the muscle formed by swinging a pick and wielding a shovel now turned to fat after so many years of indoor work. He looked at Ki from eyes slitted behind creased, drooping lids.

"I wouldn't call it crazy," Ki said mildly, pulling up his horse beside the mine manager's. "Miss Starbuck's concerned about the way production's been falling off lately. She thinks it's time to look for a fresh lode."

"Well, that's her privilege," Coats grunted. "But as far as I'm concerned, she'd be better off letting me send out a prospector or two instead of wasting time up in the air like she's planning on doing."

Ki and Coats were riding through the forest of thinly spaced ponderosa and piñon trees that covered the low canyon-cut hills northeast of the Starbuck mine. Ki went on, "If you've never been up in a balloon, you can't understand how much you can see from up above."

"You can't see what's under the ground!" Coats protested.

"I didn't suggest that you could," Ki agreed. "But you can compare ground contours and ledge formations, and spot those that have similarities to areas where silver lodes have been found before."

"I can see all I need to with my feet on the ground or my butt in a saddle," Coats replied. "But I guess if Miss Starbuck wants to waste her time and money on a fool's dream, it's up to her to decide."

"Yes, it is," Ki said. "Now, you know this territory better than I do. Where's the best place to send Sanders up in his balloon to get a view of the most promising area?"

"Just put your finger on a map anyplace between here and line back to the road from Silver City to Santa Rita," Coats replied after a moment's thought. "Just about all of it's been prospected before, but I guess you know that."

Ki nodded. "Yes, but from what I've heard, all the silver is in small pockets, like it is in the Starbuck mine. Nobody's ever found the main lode."

"Damn small wonder!" the mine manager snorted. "What's come out has mostly been dug by the Indians. They've been taking little scrapings of silver ore out of this part of the country and smelting it in their little backyard 'dobe furnaces as long as anybody can remember."

"But nobody's ever found a main lode?"

"Not yet. And it sure ain't been because they didn't try to. If this crazy idea Miss Starbuck's got turns out to be any good, maybe it'd turn up a lode nobody's run into yet, but I sure don't see much chance of it."

"I'm sure Jessie has figured the chances out for herself," Ki said quietly. "And I think I've seen all I need to now."

"Can we get on back to the mine, then?" Coats asked. "It's going to get dark fast soon as the sun drops below them mountains, and Miss Starbuck might need me to help her find whatever she's looking for in my ledgers."

When Ki and Coats reached the mine office, Jessie was

just putting the ledgers back in their cabinet.

"I hope you've found a good place for Ted to start from, Ki," she said, pushing the last ledger on the shelf and closing the cabinet door. "He'll be ready to go up tomorrow."

"I suppose the place Coats showed me is as good as any to start from," Ki replied. "I can take Ted and his crew out there in the morning and let him pick the place where he'll launch the balloon to get the best wind drift."

"Then we might as well go back to town," Jessie said. "I think I've seen all I need to of Dan's ledgers." She turned to the mine manager and went on, "Tomorrow or the next day, I'll want to get your original copies of the reports from the Santa Rita assay office and go over them with you."

"But I sent you copies of all those reports not more'n two or three weeks ago," Coats said, frowning.

"I know, and I've looked at them. But I'd like to see the original assay reports, just the same."

"Oh, sure." Coats nodded. "Whenever you say, Miss Starbuck. If you don't want to wait till tomorrow, I'll get them out for you right now. It'll only take a minute."

"Tomorrow's soon enough," Jessie told him. "At the moment, I'm anxious to get back to town and see if I need to do anything to help the balloonists. I want to be sure they're ready to go up tomorrow."

As they rode along the winding tree-lined road toward town in the last dimming rays of sunset, Jessie told Ki, "From the quick look I took, the ledgers are all in order, but there's something about them that still bothers me."

"And you couldn't put your finger on it?"

"I'm not sure yet." Jessie paused for a moment, then went on, speaking slowly and thoughtfully. "The one odd thing that struck me might not mean anything. At least it doesn't to me, but perhaps it will to you."

"Remember what the barrel is supposed to have told the box." Ki smiled, trying to lighten Jessie's mood. "Two heads are better than one. Go ahead, maybe I can help you puzzle it out."

Jessie did not reply until they'd ridden on for a moment in silence, then she said, "If the silver lode is petering out, I'd think that the mine ought to produce less copper and gold as well. But the ledgers don't show any change. That's why I want to look at the assay-office reports."

This time it was Ki who rode on for a silent moment before he said slowly, "I still remember what I learned when we were having trouble with the copper diggings up in Montana, Jessie. Silver and copper and gold ores can be mixed in the same lode, but when they are, they're always just traces. I don't see that it would make any difference how much of the trace metals are mixed in with the silver."

"Maybe it doesn't," she agreed. "But that's the only thing I saw in the mine ledgers that struck me as being odd."

"Well, a closer look might—"

Ki broke off as a rifle barked from the trees beside the road and a slug whined its menacing high-pitched note as it passed between him and Jessie.

Accustomed to reacting instantly to unexpected attacks, neither of them needed to speak. Jessie twitched Sun's reins and the big palomino whirled quickly, starting for the thin cover of the trees that lined the road.

Ki was as swift to act as Jessie had been. He reined his pony in the same direction Jessie was taking, heading for cover, but rode at an angle to her path. They were using a long-standing maneuver they'd worked out, its purpose to force an unseen attacker to choose one or the other as a target. Though the delay they gained amounted to only a fraction of a second, the splinter of time lost by a sniper in

67

deciding which of them to select was usually enough to give both of them the time needed to escape safely.

This time was no exception. The slug from the hidden rifleman's third shot whined over Jessie's head as Sun spurted down the long grade slanting from the road. Sparse as the cover was on the downslope, Jessie managed to spot a copse of stunted piñon trees just ahead and reined the big palomino into it.

Ki in the meantime had swerved away from the road and reined his mount onto a short abrupt drop that took him behind a rock outcrop well below the level ground on which the road ran.

Off the road, the shadows of the gathering night were deeper. Jessie in her copse of trees and Ki behind the rock shoulder waited for another shot, but none came. Instead they heard the grating of hoofbeats from the upslope. They could follow the sniper's movements almost as easily by the thudding of his mount's hooves as they could have if they'd been able to see him. There were a few muffled clomps of his horse's hooves as he gained the road, then the rapid pattering of hoofbeats as he spurred away.

"Are we going after him?" Ki called into the gloom, sure that Jessie was within earshot.

"It wouldn't do us much good," she replied. "By the time we get back up the grade, he'll have such a start on us that we'd never be able to catch up with him. Even if we got close, he could still slip away from us in the dark."

Ki nudged his horse into motion and twitched the reins to return to the road. He heard Sun's hooves close by, then he was on the edge of the road, with Jessie just behind him.

"Did you get the same idea that came to me?" she asked.

"I've got two ideas," Ki replied as they started toward

Silver City. "One is that Dan Coats started from the mine and cut across country to get here before we did. The other is that some outlaw who just happened to be around heard us coming along the road and decided he might pick up some easy money by bushwacking us."

"I hadn't thought about an outlaw," Jessie told him. "It could've been one, I suppose, but it's a long shot at best. If I wanted to make this a betting matter, I'd put a bigger bet on it being Coats who shot at us."

"He's the only one we know around here who'd have any reason to ambush us," Ki agreed. "He knew we'd take the road to town, and I'm sure he'd be able to take a straight course across country that'd get him here faster than we did. I'm inclined to agree with you, Jessie. The thing to decide now is what to do about it."

"Suppose we change our plans a little bit," she suggested. "As long as you and I are here, Coats is going to be uneasy. If I'm right, and he has been juggling the mine's books, he won't risk touching them while we're here. But if I let him know that I'm going up in the balloon with Ted, he's going to get very busy trying to cover up his thefts before I start looking at the ledgers again."

"And I'll be keeping an eye on him, of course."

Jessie nodded. "You're better at that than I am, Ki. I'm not good at making myself invisible, the way you are."

"I can go back to the mine right now, if you want me to, and start watching him," Ki offered.

"Even if Coats is still there, I doubt that he'd try to do anything tonight, and we need to talk about our new plans with Ted. Besides, if you're as hungry as I am, we'll both be better able to work out a plan after we've eaten."

Jessie and Ki were almost through with their meal when Will Talley came into the hotel dining room. He stopped

69

just inside the door to flick his eyes around the room. He saw Jessie and made a beeline to the table where she and Ki were sitting.

"Miss Starbuck," he said, doffing his hat. "I was wondering if I might not run into you here. Do you mind if I sit down with you?"

"Why—not at all," Jessie replied, hiding her surprise. "I was intending to look in at your office later, but running into you now will save me bothering you while you're busy with other things."

"I hope you haven't been having trouble at the mine." The marshal frowned. "It's inside my jurisdiction, too, you know."

"How does that happen?" she asked. "I thought the town marshal's authority stopped at the town limits."

"Technically, it does. But the sheriff over at Santa Rita has had trouble keeping a deputy there, so he's deputized me until he can find another man."

"Then you're the one I should be talking to," Jessie said. "While Ki and I were riding back to town from the mine, somebody ambushed us and tried to kill us."

"The hell—" Talley started, stopped short, and said, "I hope you'll excuse my swearing, ma'am. I didn't—"

Jessie suppressed the smile that started twitching her lips and said dryly, "I live on a ranch, Marshal Talley. I've heard the word before."

"Yes, ma'am." Talley nodded, then went on, "If you'll tell me who you think it might've been that ambushed you, Miss Starbuck, I'll get on their trail and I won't give up until I catch them!"

Chapter 7

"At least we're going to have a good day for our trial run," Jessie told Ki as she looked past the swelling bag of the balloon at the sky.

"It looks that way," he agreed.

They were standing beside the basket of the balloon in the little clearing Ted Sanders had chosen for their first ascent after scouting the area around the Starbuck mine. The clearing was bordered by a stand of wide-spaced ponderosa pines rising between scattered clusters of low-growing piñons. A gently rising hillock filled the fifty or sixty yard circular area, and the balloon was staked at the rounded top of the rise.

Ted Sanders was in the basket, checking its scanty equipment for the second time since they'd started inflating the big balloon. Tim O'Brien was hunkered down beside a small, bright fire at one side of the clearing, feeding it with fast-burning dry piñon branches. The wagon stood beyond him at the edge of the trees, Sun and Ki's mustang hitched to one of its wheels.

Nora, her hands encased in thick mitts, stood beside the basket, holding the hot outlet of the air duct in line with the bag's spout. The sections of the big metal pipe, supported by three sets of branches lashed into X's, stretched back to the fire Tim was looking after.

Wisps of hot air shimmered in the small gap between the fire and the duct's hood, and now and then a thin wisp of smoke escaped through the gap between the end of the duct and the air bag's dangling spout. The golden hues of sunrise were almost gone by now, and the sky was clear and blue except for an almost invisible sheen of filmy white on the western horizon, and even this distant haze was rapidly dissipating as the sun's rays reached it.

"Not a real cloud anywhere in sight," Jessie went on.

"I'd like it better if there were a few clouds scattered here and there," Sanders said, looking around from the basket. "They'd give me a hint about what the air currents are like at different levels."

"That hadn't occurred to me, Ted," Jessie observed. "Will it bother you if you can't tell how high to go to find a wind that's blowing in the right direction?"

Ted shook his head. "It's not all that important, Jessie. What I meant is that a sky as absolutely clear as this one might make us waste a little time seesawing up and down while we look for the current moving in the direction we want to go."

"Well, time's not really that important," Jessie said. "We've got the whole day ahead of us, and I don't mind spending most of it in the sky."

"It'll only be a few minutes before you'll be up there," Nora volunteered. "The bag's just about ready now. It needs to be filled a bit more than usual. The upper air's still cool this early in the day, and the sun's not as hot as it will be later."

Ki looked up at the swelling bag. It was now tugging at its anchor rope, its glossy fabric almost taut. He asked Ted, "You're sure you won't need me to help down here?"

"There's nothing you could do on the ground except keep Nora and Tim company," the balloonist replied.

"They'll be following us with the wagon, if you want to go along with them."

"Ballooning's still strange to me," Ki said. "I don't know whether I'd be helpful, or just get in their way."

"If you get in the way, Tim or Nora will tell you fast enough." Ted smiled. "But suit yourself, Ki. Jessie's told me the kind of ground formation she's looking for, and as soon as we find an upper air current that's moving in the right direction I'll level the balloon off and we'll start drifting. With me to help her read the ground signs we shouldn't be left aloft more than a couple of hours."

"I'll take care of my business at the mine while you're up above, then. Every now and then I'll step out of the office and look up, and when I see you coming down I'll join you." Turning to Jessie, Ki went on, "Just as soon as you're in the air, I'll get on with that job we talked about."

"Good." She nodded. "Have you figured out a way to find out what we need to know without raising any suspicions?"

"I'm still working on a plan for that, Jessie. But don't worry, I'll have some sort of scheme ready before I get to the mine."

"I'm sure you will," Jessie agreed. "And I hope I'm wrong about Coats, but my instinct tells me I'm not. Of course—" She stopped short as Ted stepped across the basket and broke in on their conversation.

"You'd better hop in with me now," he told Jessie. "By the time you get settled, we'll be ready to go up."

Jessie vaulted into the basket in a single lithe move. Nora had already lifted the duct away and was lowering it to the ground. Ted grasped the end of the tether rope that dangled from a slipknot and yanked it. The knot slipped out and the basket tilted slightly, swayed, and lifted a few inches.

73

Ted motioned for Jessie to get into the corner opposite him. She moved into place and grasped the wicker rim as he tossed the end of the anchor rope to Nora. The balloon was rising now, but Jessie's sensation was that the big bag was hovering motionless while the ground dropped steadily away.

Her feeling persisted even when the basket rose above the treetops and she saw the green saw-toothed peaks of mountains rise to eye level. Whether Jessie looked northwest toward the mountains or southeast where the arid ocher plains fell away into the endless distance, she still had the sensation that the balloon itself was hovering motionless and the ground below was falling away from it. The illusion continued as the balloon rose for several minutes and the earth began taking on the shape of a shallow circular saucer that slowly grew bigger around its rim.

Jessie looked directly down over the edge of the basket. Ki, Nora, and Ted had moved to the top of the hillock in the center of the clearing, and she saw their faces as featureless white blobs, their bodies as lumps against the brown soil.

"We haven't moved very much in any direction, have we?" she asked Ted.

"No. We've lost the ground wind now, even though there wasn't very much of it to start with. But we're rising faster all the time now that the sun's full on the bag, and I'll just let us go on up until we find a current that'll carry us in the direction you want to go."

"Aren't we already higher than we were when you took me up at the Circle Star?"

"Quite a bit. And it looks like we'll have to go still higher before we'll get into any kind of wind current. I don't remember that I've ever gone up before in such quiet air."

74

"Is that good or bad?"

"It depends on how you want to look at it. You'll see a lot more ground area without moving, but what you see below won't be as easy to identify as it would be if were lower."

"At least it's not—" Jessie said, but before she'd finished what she was about to say the balloon above them heeled over, whirling the basket, then suddenly jerking it into a steep slant.

Jessie reacted quickly, for her years of living with the possibility that danger was just in the offing had honed her reflexes to razor sharpness. She tightened her grip on the edge of the basket and braced her feet on its floor. Almost before the basket had settled to its new angle she had locked herself into the corner, hunkering down with her feet pushed against the bottom and her hands locked over the rim. Braced as she was, Jessie was sure that further gyrations of the basket could not dislodge her easily.

Ted had not been as quick to react, or as fortunate. When the basket tilted he'd been standing away from the sides, and its sudden jerk sent him sprawling in the bottom. As the big bag above them had continued to heel over, dragging the basket into a steeper angle, he'd been thrown in a heap against the basket's side. Recovering quickly from his sprawl, Ted reached up and locked his hands over the rim, braced his feet, and pulled himself up. He did not try to stand upright, but leaned back against the side of the basket.

As the balloon continued to rise, the ropes attaching it to the net that enclosed the bag slowly straightened out, but the force of the stratum of flowing wind they'd entered was so great that the basket still maintained its slant as the swift wind ragged the balloon with it.

"What happened to us, Ted?" Jessie asked as the balloonist righted himself and peered over the basket rim.

"We're in a levanter," he replied. Then, when he saw from her still-puzzled expression that the word meant nothing to her, he explained, "That's what balloonists call an exceptionally strong upper air current like the one we're in now."

"Is it dangerous?" she asked, her voice as calm as though she were asking him to tell her the time of day.

"Not unless we get carried up a lot higher than we are now, or unless we start dropping and run into a cross-current."

"What happens then?"

"Very unpleasant things that I don't even like to think about."

"You might as well tell me, Ted. I'd rather know in advance what to expect than to be taken by surprise."

After a moment's hesitation, Ted replied, "If we drop into a crosscurrent, or an opposing wind, the basket might be torn away from the bag. Or the bag itself might collapse."

"You were right." Jessie nodded. "I don't find either of those things very pleasant to think about."

"I've been caught twice in levanters, Jessie, and both times I've been lucky. Neither of them was anywhere near this strong. I don't really know what to expect."

"Isn't there a way for you to get us out of it?"

"None that I know of."

"You mean that we can't go up or down to get out of this awful wind?"

"Changing altitude in a levanter might be the most dangerous thing we could do," he replied soberly. "We're not in any real danger as long as we're just being carried along this way. If I try to change anything—well, I don't know what might happen."

76

"Surely you've talked to other balloonists who've been in this same situation, Ted. Didn't you get some ideas from them?"

"This isn't something that happens very often, Jessie. We don't know much about this kind of wind yet." His voice grew grim as he went on, "Every balloonist I know speculates about levanters, but there've only been a few who've survived being caught in a bad one.

"And this is a bad one?"

"Based on my limited experience, I'd say it is."

"What do we do, then?"

"Nothing. Except hang tight to the basket, of course."

"But we're being carried away from the mine!"

"Yes. And we'll go on being carried away until the wind dies down."

"You don't know how long that will take?" Jessie asked.

"I wish I could tell you I did, but I'd be lying," Ted replied ruefully. "Nobody knows enough about the upper air to answer many questions about it. A few years from now, when there are more balloons and balloonists, we may know at least a few more of the answers, including the reasons why winds up this high behave the way they do."

"That's not much help to us right this minute, is it?" Jessie asked.

"None at all. The only thing we can do is hang on to the basket and let the wind carry us until it dies down."

"There's not any way to judge how fast we're going, either, I suppose?" she asked.

"Well, I can make a pretty fair guess just by watching the ground. I'll pick out a landmark ahead of our course and estimate how far it is, then a little arithmetic will give us our approximate speed. I've never tried it in a balloon that's moving as fast as we are now, but I think I can come pretty close."

Gripping the basket rim tightly, Ted peered over. He watched the ground for a few moments, then turned back to Jessie.

"As close as I can tell, we're moving at something like seventy miles an hour, maybe a little faster."

"But that's faster than a train can go, Ted!"

"Yes, I know. And it's a lot faster than I've ever moved in a balloon before."

Jessie shielded her eyes and glanced at the sun to get an idea of the direction in which they were moving. Looking back at Ted, she said, "We're going south and a bit to the east. If we're really going as fast as you estimated, we'll be blown across the border into Mexico in a little more than an hour!"

"Let's hope the levanter dies away before then," Ted said. "But if it doesn't, we may just have to land in Mexico."

Ki and his companions in the clearing had been watching the balloon when it was caught up by the vicious wind. He saw the bag heel over, then watched it pick up speed as it started moving across the sky. From the angle at which he was looking, the balloon's movement seemed to be much slower than it actually was. Not until he looked at Nora and Tim and saw the worried frowns they wore did Ki realize that something was badly amiss.

"They're not going in the direction Jessie planned," he said, looking from Nora to Tim O'Brien, reading the concern reflected in their faces. "And from the way you look and act, I'm sure that something's gone wrong."

Nora started to reply, but couldn't bring out the words she was seeking. She looked at her father and raised her eyebrows questioningly.

"It's too early to worry, Ki," O'Brien said. "They've

been caught by a bad wind up aloft. It's what balloonists call a levanter." He stopped uncertainly, his brow puckered in a worried frown, then added, "There's no way Ted can get out of it safely. All they can do is let the levanter carry them until it dies away."

"They're already eight or ten miles from here," Ki said, looking up again at the balloon. "Hadn't we better start following them to help them land?"

"We wouldn't have a chance of keeping up with them," Nora said quickly. "They're moving in a straight line and going a lot faster than the wagon could."

"We can't just stand here and watch them disappear!" Ki objected. "They'll need your help to get back down to earth!"

"Ted's a very good balloonist," Nora said quickly. "He can land the balloon without help. And you can see for yourself that we don't have a chance in the world of catching up with them."

"Not with the wagon," Ki agreed reluctantly. "But the new railroad grade's only a few miles from the foothills. I might have a chance to keep them in sight if I ride Sun."

"Ki, there's not a horse alive that can catch up with that balloon," Tim objected. "It's moving as fast as a railroad train."

"Then I'll have to follow it in a railroad train," Ki shot back. "The balloon will be in sight of the tracks unless the wind up above changes a great deal. I'll charter a train with just an engine and one car and load Sun and the wagon on it. We'll be moving almost as fast as the balloon."

"But if the wind does change and carry the bag in a different direction, you could lose sight of it in just a few minutes," Tim pointed out.

"As long as it's in the air, we've got a chance to see it," Ki retorted. "I know a little bit about the country Jessie and

Ted are passing over. It's as flat as a tabletop except for an occasional mesa or valley."

Nora turned to her father and said, "Ki's right, Da. We'd better get the wagon hitched up as fast as we can and go with him. We won't be able to keep up, but if the country's as flat as he says, we can follow him and try to keep him in sight. And once we get to the railroad—"

"All right," O'Brien agreed. He started to walk slowly toward the wagon. "We'll do our best, lass. And if we're going to be able to keep the balloon in sight, we'd best get moving. You see to the gear; I'll hitch up the wagon."

"I'll start right now," Ki told them. He gazed up at the balloon again. It looked like a child's toy now, and was still sweeping through the cloudless sky in a straight line to the southeast. "We'll be out of the mountains after about four miles, and the the new railroad grade is only a little way beyond the foothills. I'll make the arrangements and wait for you there."

Before either Tim or Nora could say anything more, Ki swung into Sun's saddle and started off at a gallop.

"How long do you think this wind will keep blowing?" Jessie asked. She and Ted were still crouched on the basket floor, and the bag was still leaning ahead of the basket. "It doesn't show any signs of dying, and we've been up here a long time."

"Not as long as you think," Ted told her. "It just seems that way."

"We've come a long way from where we started, though."

"Yes, and we might have to go quite a way farther before it'll be safe to descend. This levanter's a really big one."

"These winds—the levanters—do they all act the same?"

"Generally they do. Nobody really knows much about them, Jessie—what causes them to form, how long they blow, things of that sort. And nobody's ever been able to measure their real speed."

"They certainly do move a balloon along. Do they die down as fast as they spring up?"

"That's something else no one's sure about."

"I don't think I've ever moved this fast before," Jessie said. "It's quite an experience."

"One that you don't want to repeat, I'm sure." Ted managed a lopsided smile. Then the smile vanished and he went on, "Now, there's one thing I'd better warn you about. We're already dropping a bit, and we'll drop still more unless I can manage to get some more hot air in the bag during the next half hour."

Jessie glanced up at the big bag. It was still leaning ahead of the basket, the spout dangling at an angle that made it impossible to reach.

"What happens if you can't put in more hot air?" she asked.

"We might drop below the bottom edge of the levanter."

"You make it sound like that would be serious," she said frowning.

"It would be. Moving as fast as we are, the balloon would very likely be torn to shreds if it dropped into an opposing air current. I don't think I need to go on and describe what would happen to the basket and to us."

"No," Jessie said soberly. "And since I don't think you're any more eager than I am to have that happen, we'd better get busy and figure out a way to keep it from happening."

Chapter 8

Pushing Sun to the big palomino's limit, Ki had kept the balloon in sight during almost two hours of wild pursuit. Even though Sun had done his best to maintain the pace Ki demanded, it was plain by now that they had no chance of winning the lopsided chase. Even Sun's great strength and stamina would fail before he could catch up with the fast-moving air bag, and the horse drawing the wagon was already faltering.

Looking back along the rough trail that threaded across the flat, desertlike plateau, Ki could see that Tim and Nora had not yet given up, even though they were almost two miles behind him by now. The balloon had not changed course, but it was a tiny spot no bigger than Ki's thumb, a mere dot in the cloudless morning sky, and pulling steadily farther away from him.

Dropping his eyes back to the ground, Ki saw the gleaming canvas of a tent city, the tents clustered around a few large, ramshackle buildings. A puff of white steam suddenly appeared above one of the structures and the black outline of a railroad locomotive emerged from behind the building. Ki realized that he'd reached the construction camp at the end of the spur being built by the Southern Pacific into Silver City.

Seeing the locomotive and the shining rails that extended south from the camp, Ki hoped that his plan would work. Twitching the reins, he headed Sun toward the camp, keeping his eyes on the distant balloon, now only a black speck against the cloudless sky.

"Charter a locomotive and boxcar!" the foreman of the Southern Pacific's railhead construction gang snorted after he'd heard Ki's request. "What in hell do you think this is? We're building track here, and what rolling stock we got is for work, not to hand over to anybody that pops up outa noplace and asks for it."

"Of course I understand that this is a construction camp and not a passenger depot," Ki said patiently. "But my need is very urgent. I will be happy to pay—"

"From the way you look, you couldn't pay for a two-for-a-nickel cigar at the commissary! Now, make yourself scarce. I got work to do."

Controlling his temper, Ki repeated, "It might be a matter of life and death! I must ask you to reconsider!"

"Reconsider my ass!" the foreman grated. He was both tall and bulky, outweighing Ki by perhaps a hundred pounds. The top of Ki's head was level with his broad shoulders.

Looking disdainfully at Ki's simple cotton blouse and trousers, his well-worn black leather vest, and the sandals he preferred in place of shoes, the railroader went on, "Even if I had any rolling stock to charter, which I don't, it looks to me like you ain't got enough money to rent a mangy workmule. Get outa here now, and take your damn jokes someplace else. I got six crews at work pushing iron to Silver City as fast as we know how to, and I ain't got time to waste on foolishness."

Keeping his growing anger in check, Ki said levelly, "I

83

have tried to make it clear to you that money is no object."

"That's easy enough to say," the railroader snapped. "Now, get on your way before I really get mad."

"I see you're unable to understand me," Ki went on regretfully. "That means I'll have to talk to your superiors."

"What superiors?" the foreman asked, his lips twitching into a grin. "I'm top dog here. The construction superintendent is the only one that gives me orders."

"Then I shall talk to him," Ki said quietly.

"You'll have to make a trip to El Paso to do it. That's where his office is. You go ahead, chase on down there, and if I get a wire from him telling me to charter you a loco and a boxcar, I'll be glad to do it. Be sure you tell him that fool yarn about a runaway balloon that somebody put you up to spin me."

"You have a telegraph wire from El Paso, then?"

"Of course we do. How—" The foreman stopped short, shook his head and went on, "Damned if you ain't got me halfway started listening to you! Now get on outa here before I throw you out on your butt!"

Still forcing himself to speak politely, almost humbly, Ki said, "Perhaps you will be good enough to show me where your telegraph office is located. I will be most happy to send a message to your superintendent myself."

"Why, you stupid goddamned Chink!" the man exploded. "Looks like the only way I'm going to get rid of you is toss you outa the yard myself!" He took a half step forward, raising his hands toward Ki as he moved. "So that's what I'm going to do!"

Ki did not seem to move fast, but suddenly he was holding the railroader's open right hand in his own. Ki's steel-hard fingertips dug into the fleshy pad between the man's thumb and forefinger, where the sensitive nerves that trans-

84

mit feelings from the fingertips come together in a cluster.

At the same time he yanked the man forward, throwing him off-balance, and twisted the hand up and around, thrusting the foreman's elbow into the soft, thin flesh of his belly just below his rib cage. Using his grip as a fulcrum and the foreman's own arm as a lever, Ki began forcing his antagonist to his knees. The railroader swung his free arm wildly, trying to drive home a roundhouse blow, but Ki evaded it with a short, quick sidewise step, at the same time digging his fingertips deeper into the nerves they were pressing.

Using his new leverage, he swung the railroader around. The blow that the man had started flailed at nothing but thin air, while the energy he'd expended launching it only served to increase the leverage Ki was exercising on his imprisoned arm.

"Damn you, that hurts!" the railroader yelled. "If you ever let go of me, I'll stomp you to a pulp!"

"I have no intention of releasing you," Ki said in his softest, most polite tone. "You will now walk with me to your telegrapher, and I will give him a message to send your superintendent."

"Like hell I will! I'll stomp you—" The foreman's threat ended in a yowl of pain as Ki dug his fingertips even deeper into the nerve center at the base of his captive's thumb. His voice thinning almost to a falsetto as the darts of fresh pain ran up his arm to his shoulder, the foreman gasped, "All right, damn you! The brass pounder's right over there, in that red boxcar on the siding."

Ki eased off a bit on the grip of his fingertips, but maintained enough pressure to remind the foreman what would happen if he tried to break free. He started for the red boxcar, the foreman sidling along beside him, still trying to pull free from Ki's digging fingertips.

A ramp slanted up from the ground to the opened sliding doors of the boxcar and Ki forced his prisoner up and into the car. The telegrapher was sprawled in a chair, half-asleep. He roused and sat up when he heard their footsteps and his jaw dropped at the sight of the bulky foreman helpless in the grip of a man half his size.

"What in hell's going on here?" the brass pounder asked.

"This damn Chink's got me where the hair's short," the foreman gasped. "He wants to send a wire to the super in El Paso."

"You want me to send it, or pull him off you?" the telegrapher asked.

Ki increased the pressure on his hapless captive's hand and the foreman quickly said, "No, damn it! He could rip my arm off before you got to him! Open your key and send whatever he says."

Puzzled but obedient, the telegrapher moved to the seat in front of his key and reached for the instrument. He looked at Ki questioningly, his brow still furrowed in surprise.

"You will start by telling the operator in El Paso that my message is for the immediate attention of your district superintendent. I want him to be at the El Paso operator's side while he is receiving what you will send," Ki told him. "I must tell you that I have some knowledge of telegraphy, and I will know at once if you try to trick me. Now, open your key and send what I have told you."

"Do it, damn it!" the foreman snapped when the telegrapher looked at him, his eyebrows raised questioningly. "This damn Chink's gonna rip my hand off if you don't."

"It's gonna make the super real mad," the telegrapher said.

"I'll square things up with the super," the foreman replied quickly. "And remember this little bastard's a lot smarter than he looks, so don't try to fool him."

Obediently, the telegrapher began fingering his instrument. Ki's knowledge of Morse code was limited, but he could catch enough of the message to know that the telegrapher was following instructions. For a moment after he'd finished sending, the key was silent, then it chattered briefly.

"Joe says that message didn't make much sense to him, but he's sending a tallow monkey to find the super anyhow," the telegrapher told the foreman. "What do I tell him when he gets there?"

Before the foreman could reply, Ki said, "You will send what I tell you, without changing a word. Do you understand?"

"Sure, sure," the man at the key answered quickly. "This ain't no business of mine, you know. I'll just follow your orders."

A very few minutes passed before the key burst into life again. The telegrapher looked a question at Ki, who nodded.

"Send this exactly as I say it," he repeated, "whether you think it makes sense or not." He waited for the telegrapher's nod of agreement, then dictated slowly: "'This message is from Jessica Starbuck. If you have any questions about my identity, wire Leland Stanford at once and he will give you any information required. I need to rent a locomotive and boxcar from your construction gang at this railhead for an emergency trip to El Paso. Cost is no object. Please act at once on this request.'"

As soon as Ki had dictated the first three or four words of the message the telegrapher had started his key to clacking. He finished transmitting Ki's message only a few seconds after Ki had stopped speaking.

87

For several minutes the telegraph key was silent, then it started clacking again. The telegrapher began scribbling on the pad of flimsies that lay on the table beside the key. As he wrote, his eyes widened, and he glanced sideways at Ki and the foreman. At last the key stopped clattering.

"Gawdamighty!" the brass pounder gasped. "Boss, you sure got something here bigger'n you can handle."

"What d'you mean?" The foreman frowned.

"Well, this fellow sure ain't no lady named Starbuck, but if he's working for her, then you better kowtow to him."

"Read the message!" Ki snapped.

"Sure." The telegrapher nodded. "Here's what the super says." Reading from the flimsy now, he went on, "'Starbuck name needs no confirmation. Glad to grant your request. If further help needed, please notify me.'"

A puzzled frown had grown on the foreman's face as he listened to the telegrapher. Twisting his head to look at Ki, he asked, "Just who the hell is this Jessica Starbuck?"

"I have the honor to work for her," Ki replied.

"Well, she sure must be some kinda high-up muckety-muck," the foreman said. Both his voice and his face showed his bewilderment.

"Hold on," the telegrapher broke in. "There's another send here that I ain't read you yet. It's from the super to you." Reading from the flimsy, he went on, "Fill without question any request Miss Starbuck makes."

His eyes wide, his face even more puzzled than it had been before, the foreman gasped gustily. Then he told Ki, "I guess your boss swings a lot more weight than I do. If you'll let go of me, I'll follow the super's orders. I won't ask no questions and I'll have a loco and boxcar ready for you in about ten minutes."

Ki nodded, his face expressionless. He released his hold on the foreman's hand and said, "Thank you. I regret that I had to use force on you, but the situation I am in left me no other choice. Oh—I'll need a ramp to load a wagon and our horses into the boxcar. And if you have a commissary here, I'll like to buy some food and supplies."

"Whatever you want," the man said, massaging his hand and arm. "I don't know what this is all about, but I aim to do like I was told to."

By the time the locomotive and boxcar were ready to roll and Ki had given the engineer and fireman their instructions, Nora and Tim had arrived in the wagon. Ki looked at the heaving sides of the horse and the streaks of lather along its jaws.

"It's a good thing the construction camp was no farther away than it was," he said. "Ten more miles and that horse would be dead."

"It's pretty well blowed, all right," Tim agreed. "But a little rest and it'll be able to keep up."

"Let's get the wagon and horses in the boxcar, then," Ki urged. "The longer we wait, the harder it's going to be to catch up with Jessie and Ted."

"There's only one thing I don't like about switching this way," Tim said as he began unhitching the horse. "A horse and wagon can change directions easy enough. That's more than you can say for a train."

"If you noticed on the way here from the Circle Star, the railroad tracks run almost as straight as a string," Ki told him. He broke off as Tim led the horse out of the wagon shafts and handed the reins to Nora. "I've been watching the balloon since we started after it. It hasn't changed course a bit, and as nearly as I can judge, it's still sailing almost parallel to the railroad tracks."

All three of them tilted their heads to look up at the sky. The balloon was so far away by now that it was barely visible.

"It looks like it's still moving in the same direction,

from what I can see." Nora frowned. "But there's never any way of knowing when the wind will change."

"We'll worry about that later," Ki told her. "Covering the ground between us and Jessie and Ted is the most important thing at the moment. As long as we can keep the balloon in sight, we can always stop the engine and go back to following with Sun and the wagon."

"Let's get started, then," she urged. "You and Da pull the wagon up the ramp. I'll lead the horses."

Less than five minutes later, the bobtail train pulled out of the construction camp and was rocking along the newly laid rails in pursuit of the balloon.

"Do you have any idea how far we've traveled, Ted?" Jessie asked. "It seems to me that we've been moving awfully fast for a long time."

"Oh, we've been pushed real fast," Ted agreed. "And the levanter's blowing just as hard as it was when we got caught in it. But it's not easy to judge speed or distance without being able to watch the ground for a few minutes."

Both Jessie and the balloonist were still crouched in the bottom of the basket, clinging to the rim. Neither the basket nor the balloon had changed its position since the levanter had caught them. The bag was still tilted at an angle, pulling the basket at the awkward slant into which it had been pulled when the first gusts of the wild wind had struck it.

"We still haven't made any plans about what we're going to do when the wind finally dies," Jessie reminded her companion.

"No. And I don't think we can plan anything, Jessie," Ted replied. "I told you, I've been caught in a levanter twice before, and the bag acted differently each time. From what I've heard from others who've been in them, there's no way of predicting how a balloon will act when it gets out of a levanter's current."

"What are we supposed to do, then?"

Ted shook his head. "I don't know. I suppose we'll just do the best thing instinctively."

"And how can we be sure we'll do what's right? Our instinct might be wrong, you know."

"Then I guess we'd better pray a little bit."

"Do you think I haven't been?" Jessie asked.

"So have I, for that matter," he admitted. "Mainly for time enough to get some more hot air into the bag. It's been deflating for quite a while now."

Jessie twisted her head to get a better view of the big air bag. Its spout was sagging now, almost limp instead of holding its rounded funnel shape. Above the spout, the bag itself was no longer taut. The ropes that encased it like a web were sunk into the fabric, and a wrinkle showed here and there on the bag's bulging form.

"Does that mean we're just going to drop like a rock?" she asked.

"Not exactly like a rock." Ted's brow was wrinkled, his expression thoughtful. He went on, "It won't be a well-controlled landing, though. Right now, the levanter's holding us up and carrying us along at the same time, like a scrap of paper or a leaf that's been picked up by a high wind. But we've been slowly losing altitude for the past quarter of an hour."

"I guess I don't know enough about balloons to notice things like that," Jessie told him. Her voice was thoughtful as she said, "I don't suppose there's anything we can do about it, is there?"

Ted shook his head. "Not right now. If the levanter fades away a little at a time, we'll be all right. If that happens, we'll just float down and make a pretty normal

91

landing. But if we drop out of it while we're still moving this fast, there's a ten-to-one chance that we'll crash."

"I don't suppose it'll be anything like being thrown from a horse?"

"Imagine being thrown out of a saddle and multiply it about a hundred times or so, depending on how far and how fast we fall."

Jessie shook her head. "I don't think my imagination is up to that, Ted. Or maybe I just don't want to think about it."

Almost before Jessie had finished speaking, the basket suddenly lurched and twirled. Both Jessie and Ted looked up at the bag of the balloon. It was losing its slant now, slowly tilting upright.

"I'm afraid you're gong to have to think about it now," Ted told Jessie. "Unless I'm very much mistaken, the levanter's getting ready to die."

Chapter 9

"Can you still see the balloon, Ki?" Nora asked as she stepped up to join him at the boxcar's open door.

Even before the bobtail train had begun moving, Ki had stationed himself in the door so he could follow the course of the balloon. By now, distance had reduced the big bag to an even smaller speck. The sun was past its zenith, and the heat-haze that forms above all arid, desertlike lands from spring to autumn was beginning to shimmer above the ground. As yet the haze had not reached the upper air, and since the balloon was the only object in the bright, cloudless sky Ki had been able to find it quickly and fix his eyes on it.

"It's getting smaller all the time, but I can see it," he told Nora. Lifting his arm, he pointed to the tiny black dot.

"Oh, yes, I see it now," she said, and turned to call Tim. "Come here, Da! The balloon's still in sight!"

Tim O'Brien was at the door almost before she'd finished speaking. Nora pointed to the little black dot. The veteran balloonist followed her finger with his eyes and, after he'd watched for a moment, nodded with satisfaction.

"That's got to be it." he said. "But if you hadn't showed me where to look, I'm not sure I'd have noticed it."

"Where something like this is concerned, you're probably a better judge of distance than I am, Tim," Ki said. "How far away do you think it is?"

"At least forty miles. Maybe fifty. It's lucky the air's so clear over this desert country, or it'd be completely out of sight," Tim replied.

Ki took his eyes off the sky long enough to lean out of the door and glance ahead of the locomotive, and as he turned his face upward again he said, "I wish I could remember just how soon this railroad line curves to the east between here and the Mexican border. I wasn't particularly interested in watching the landscape when we were on the way to Silver City."

"I was," Nora volunteered. "It's the first time I've been in this part of the country. I remembered noticing how gently the railroad track was curving, and I'm almost sure that it straightened out and started north about twenty miles south of where we are now. What're you thinking about, Ki?"

"We're moving in almost the same direction the balloon is right now," Ki said thoughtfully. "But as soon as we get to the place where that long curve starts, we'll be going east, and we'll be moving away from it."

"When that happens we'll have to get off the train and start trying to follow it with the wagon," Tim said. Then he added with a frown, "But we won't be able to travel as fast in the wagon."

Ki nodded. "If we can still see it, that is. It's a long way off now, and we might not be able to keep it in sight."

"We've got to, Ki!" Nora said. "Once we lost it, we may not be able to find it again. It looks terribly small now."

"Suppose you and Tim stay here and watch the balloon, Nora," Ki suggested. "I'll go up to the locomotive and tell

94

the engineer to stop as soon as the track begins curving east."

Swinging himself up by the grab bar beside the door, Ki got on top of the boxcar, jumped into the tender, and hobbled over the chunks of coal to the engine. Both the fireman and engineer turned when he leaped from the tender and landed between them on the floor of the cab.

Raising his voice to be heard above the rush of wind and the roaring of the firebox, Ki asked the engineer, "How far ahead do the tracks turn to the east?"

"About twelve miles," the engineer answered. "But the line don't go due east, it's more like to the southeast."

"Wherever the rails start east, that's where we'll stop and get off," Ki told him. "If we headed that way, we'd be going in the wrong direction."

"You mean you'll be leaving the train for good?" the engineer asked, his voice puzzled.

"Of course." Ki nodded. "I just told you, we've got to continue due south."

"You ain't making much of a trip," the fireman observed.

"Maybe not, but it's saving us a couple of hours of horseback traveling," Ki pointed out.

"What're we supposed to do after you get off?" the engineer asked. "Wait for you, go on ahead, or back up to the railhead?"

"Didn't you get any orders before you left?"

Shaking his head, the engineer replied, "Not what I'd call real train orders. All the king snipe told us before we pulled out of the yard was to get up steam fast and highball when you gave the word, and then do whatever you said for us to."

"If that's the case, then you might as well go back after we've unloaded," Ki told the engineer.

95

"Not that it's any of my business," the engineer said, a bewildered look on his face, "but do you mind telling me why you changed your mind so fast?"

"Of course not," Ki answered. "The balloon we're chasing is heading south, and we'll lose sight of it if we turn east."

"Wait a minute, mister," the fireman broke in, his voice heavy with disbelief. "Did I hear you rightly? You did say you're chasing a balloon, didn't you?"

"That's right," Ki said.

"Then how come we ain't seen it?" the fireman asked.

"Because it's too far away."

"But you can see it?"

"Of course. I know where to look, though, or I wouldn't notice it myself," Ki explained. "It's not only a long way off, it's very high up in the air as well."

"You mind showing me where it is? I'd like mighty well to get a look at it," the fireman said.

"Step over here, then," Ki told him, and moved to the right-hand side of the cab.

The fireman followed him and Ki swept the sky with his eyes, looking for the faint speck to which the balloon had been reduced in size. But he could not see the balloon, though he was sure he was looking at exactly the place where the tiny dot had been only moments before, when he'd moved up to the engine. He swept the blue canopy of the heavens with squinted eyes, trying in vain to catch sight of the little speck of black. Everywhere he looked, the sky was totally clear except for the sun, which now hung between the zenith and the horizon.

Turning to the fireman, Ki said, "That just proves what I was telling you. I looked away from the sky when I left the boxcar, and now I've lost sight of it and can't find it again."

"You're real sure you was looking at a balloon?" the fireman asked, skepticism heavy in his voice.

"I'm sure." Ki nodded. "And I'd better get back and see if the others have lost sight of it, too."

"What about us?" the engineer asked as Ki started to turn away. "You still want us to keep going till we hit the place where the rails swing east?"

"That's the only thing I can see to do," Ki said. "We'll unload the horses and wagon there and start in the direction where the balloon was when we saw it last. Now, I've got to get back to the boxcar and see if the others can still see that balloon!"

Even before he swung through the boxcar door, Ki could tell that Nora and Tim had lost sight of the balloon at about the same time he had. They were no longer gazing at a fixed point in the distance, but were moving their heads slowly from side to side, searching the sky above the horizon with their eyes.

"You've lost it, too, haven't you?" he asked.

"Just a few minutes after you started to the locomotive," Nora told him. "We didn't take our eyes off it for a minute, Ki, but suddenly it just wasn't there any more."

"My guess is that the levanter broke up," Tim volunteered. "It lasted longer than any I've ever heard about."

"What effect would that have on the balloon?" Ki frowned.

Shaking his head slowly, Tim replied, "Why, it'd go down. It's been aloft such a long time that there wouldn't be enough hot air in the bag to keep it floating."

"Would it fall fast?"

"That's a question I can't answer, Ki. I'd say it depends on a lot of things, like how warm the air is up above the ground and what kind of wind currents they run into as the bag goes down. But don't worry, Ted's a good balloonist. I

97

trained him myself. He'll know how to handle things."

"I hope you're right, Tim," Ki said slowly. "I really hope you're right."

When Ted announced that the levanter was about to die, Jessie instinctively glanced up at the air bag. It was almost directly above the basket now, and the basket itself was returning to an even keel. When the slant of the bottom leveled off enough to make standing possible Ted stood up, and Jessie got to her feet as well. She looked over the side and was startled to see that the ground seemed to be slowly rising to meet them. The illusion lasted only a few seconds and she turned back to Ted.

"I don't suppose we've got time to put more air in the bag?" she asked.

Ted shook his head. "We'll be on the ground before I could do anything much. Even if I did get the calcium chloride generator set up, there wouldn't be enough time for it to generate enough hot air to keep us afloat. But there's still enough hot air in the bag to keep us from falling too fast, so we shouldn't hit hard when we finally do land."

"It'll be a rougher landing than the one we made when I went up at the Circle Star, won't it?"

"Oh, sure." Ted's voice was calm and level. "We won't have Tim and Nora on the ground, snubbing a landing rope to bring us down gently."

"Tell me what to do, then," Jessie said. Her voice was as calm as Ted's. "I don't want to make any mistakes."

"There's only one thing we can do, Jessie," Ted replied. "We'll just have to wait until we're almost on the ground, then jump out of the basket before it hits. Then we'll have to grab the landing rope in time to keep the balloon from getting away from us. Do you think you can do that?"

In spite of what they were facing, Jessie smiled. "I can handle the rope part. I've dropped enough loops to know how to grab one and hold on. And it's easy to see that you've never been on a ranch, Ted, or thrown by a horse. I've hit the ground more times than I can count, getting tossed off wild mustangs we were breaking on the Circle Star."

"You'll know how to cushion a fall, then?"

"Of course. I'll try to land on my feet, and if I can't, I'll go limp and hit the ground relaxed."

Ted nodded. "I'm satisfied."

He glanced over the side of the basket. While they'd been talking, the balloon had been dropping slowly but steadily, and the ground was now only a hundred feet or so below them. They were still drifting, but the light surface breeze they'd picked up as the bag descended was now carrying them to the west.

Looking around, all that Ted could see was baked yellow earth, scattered clumps of olive-green cactus, a few straggling mesquite trees, and the rough brownish humps of rock formations that occasionally broke the surface of the soil. His range of vision was limited now, and he found himself wishing that he'd had a chance to study the terrain while they were higher, to spot landmarks that might have been helpful. He turned back to Jessie and saw that she, too, was studying the ground.

"Does any of this country look familiar to you?" he asked.

"Not at all. But there are hundreds of miles that look just alike in this part of the Southwest, Ted."

"Then you don't have any more idea than I do about where we are?"

"My guess, since we've been in the air so long and moving as fast as we were until a few minutes ago, is that we're either near the southern border of New Mexico, or we've already passed over it."

"That would put us in Mexico, then." Ted frowned. "If we are over the border, would we be near a town?"

"None that I can think of. Deming's behind us by now, and the only other town reasonably close is El Paso, but I'm sure we're pretty far west of it, maybe a bit south-west."

"You'd think there'd at least be a trail somewhere."

"When there's no place to go to or come from, there's not much reason for anybody to beat a trail," Jessie pointed out.

Ted forced a smile that was somewhat less than cheerful. Gesturing toward the ground, he said, "We can worry about where we are after we land. Now, are you sure you know what to do?"

"Jump out just before we hit," Jessie replied.

"That's right." Bending down, Ted quickly pulled the ends of the ties that held the big coil in place and picked it up. He went on, "I'm going to toss this out now. It'll trail behind us and I'll grab it as soon as I can after we're on the ground."

"Don't you want me to grab it, too?"

"Yes, of course. The balloon will start going back up as soon as our weight's out of the basket, and we can't afford to let it get away."

Ted broke off long enough to throw the coil of rope out of the basket. It sailed a few feet as it fell and began unrolling, snaking along the ground behind the slowly moving basket.

By this time the ground was only a dozen feet below the bottom of the basket. Gripping the rim with both hands, Ted nodded to Jessie. She took hold of the rim as well and braced herself to jump. Ted's eyes were fixed on the ground as the balloon continued to settle slowly. When it seemed to Jessie that they were about to scrape the sandy ocher soil, Ted vaulted over the rim.

Jessie did not wait to see him land, but leaped up, levered her body over the rim, and cleared the basket with a lithe twist in midair. Her feet thudded on the sunbaked soil. She stumbled once, caught her balance, and ran the few steps that took her to the rope.

Freed of their weight, the balloon began rising again before Jessie could grasp the snaking rope. Ted was running after the slowly lifting bag, moving up the rope hand over hand, but it grew taut quickly and for a moment Jessie thought that he was going to be lifted off his feet. Then she got her hands on the rope and added her weight and strength to Ted's. The rope tightened and the balloon swayed gently above their heads, then it stopped and hung motionless while they held the rope snubbed and caught their breath. The heat into which they'd dropped was making both of them sweat profusely.

"All we need now is something to tie to," Ted said. "I looked for a tree or a bush while we were coming down, but as far as I could see there wasn't anything we could use."

"No, the desert's not famous for growing trees or shrubs," Jessie replied. She scanned the barren landscape for a moment, then went on, pointing to a thin, dark line that rose a few inches above the yellow soil about a hundred yards away. "All I can see is that rock outcrop over there."

"If that's all there is, we'll just have to figure out a way to use it, then. Come on, let's lead the bag over and see what we can work out."

They moved slowly toward the rock outcrop, the bottom of the basket floating six or eight feet above their heads and the bag slanting a bit as they walked. Jessie was surprised at the resistance the balloon offered even without being fully inflated. It strained constantly at the rope, as though eager to soar aloft again.

"I didn't realize how much lifting power your balloon has, even with most of the hot air gone," she told Ted as they inched along with short, quick steps. "It'd take one of us up right now, wouldn't it?"

"This desert isn't the coolest spot in the world, Jessie," Ted replied. "It's hot enough here on the ground for the sun to keep the air that's already in the bag at a pretty high temperature. But to get enough lift to take both of us aloft and keep us there, I'll have to add more hot air."

"If it had much more lift, we'd have trouble holding it down, though."

"Of course we would. I don't suppose you noticed, but there's a two-sheaf block in the mooring rope I use when I'm going up with a passenger. If it weren't for that, I'd need a half-dozen men instead of just Tim and Nora to hold the bag down when it's fully inflated and ready to go up."

"Without them and the wagon, how are we going to get the balloon out of here, Ted?"

"That's what I've been thinking about since we got on the ground," he replied. "A lot's going to depend on what we find when we get to that rock outcrop. I'm hoping we'll be able to find a snag of some kind that we can get the rope around, and that it will be solid enough to hold the bag on the ground while I reinflate it."

Jessie's jaw dropped. She asked. "You mean we're going to try to sail out of here?"

"Can you think of any other way to get out? Once we're in the air, I can pick up a current that'll take us in almost any direction we want to go. We might even find a town within an hour or two after we're aloft."

"I haven't gotten used to the idea of traveling through the air, Ted. When I think about going somewhere, all that occurs to me is to walk or ride a horse or take a train. I just had the idea you wanted a safe place to tether the balloon while you let the air out of it, and then we'd start walking."

Ted shook his head. "We could be fifty to a hundred miles from anywhere, Jessie. We might not find a spring or stream, and from the glimpse I got during those last minutes when we were coming down, there's no town or ranch or any sign of water for at least twenty miles in any direction."

"You've got that big can of water in the basket, haven't you?" Jessie asked. "That would be enough to last two or three days if we were careful."

"It probably would. But I'll need every drop of that water to activate the calcium chloride, and to keep us in the air."

"We'll save it for that, of course," Jessie agreed quickly. "Now, let's see if we can find a place on that rock ledge where we can tie that balloon while you put more hot air into it." She glanced at the sun, still high in the western sky.

Ted followed her gaze and said, "We've got plenty of time. It'll only take an hour or so to get the bag filled again. Then we'll be aloft and moving, with all our troubles behind us."

"That can't be too soon to suit me," Jessie told him. They were within a few yards of the rock outcrop now, and she ran her eyes along its jagged rim, then found what she'd been looking for. "Right there, Ted," she said, pointing to a deep cleft in a thick seam of rock, where a crack ran back for several feet almost horizontally to the ground. "I'm sure that will hold the bag without breaking off."

Ted studied the deep crevice for a moment and nodded.

103

"It looks stout enough to me." He was forming a loop in the rope as he spoke. Slipping the loop into the crack, he pulled it tight, then said over his shoulder to Jessie, "Let go, now. Even if the rope slips or the rock spur breaks off, I can hold the bag down long enough for you to get hold of the rope again."

Jessie released the rope and took a half step backward. The loop around the rock spur held as the rope grew taut when the lift of the air bag pulled against it.

"It looks safe enough to me," she agreed.

"Yes. It'll be fine. Now I'll get in the basket and start the calcium chloride working. We'll have to wait an hour or so for enough more hot air to be added to what's already in the bag, but we'll still have a lot of daylight left even then."

"Then I'm going to stretch out in the shade of the balloon and have a nap," Jessie said. "Call me if you need help."

Jessie had no idea how long she'd dozed before she woke with a start. The rhythmic thud of hoofbeats was reverberating in the hard-baked earth under her head. She sat up, glancing at the balloon. The back of Ted's head was visible above the rim of the basket, but the drumming of hoofbeats drew her attention away from the bag.

A dozen riders, galloping fast, their faces invisible in the shade cast by their wide-brimmed sombreros, were less than a hundred yards away from the balloon and closing the gap quickly. Jessie could see that all of them carried rifles, and her intuition told her that they meant trouble.

Leaping to her feet, she called, "Ted! There's a bunch of men coming, and they don't look friendly!"

Ted stood up in the basket and looked at the horsemen. Jessie drew her Colt, her free hand going to the shell loops in her belt to pull out cartridges for reloading. She let the revolver dangle at her side, not wanting to risk an unfriendly gesture. By now the riders were within a dozen yards of the balloon. They spread quickly into a half-moon formation and reined in. One of them pulled ahead, his rifle held in the crook of his elbow.

"Levanten sus manos!" he called, his voice harshly commanding. When neither Jessie nor Ted moved, he lifted the rifle barrel to cover them. *"Ay! Gringos!"* he snorted, then added quickly, "Take up your hands! Quick, or we shoot!"

Chapter 10

"I'd feel a lot better if we had another keg just like this one," Ki commented as he and Tim lifted the twenty-gallon barrel and deposited it in the wagon. "I've never been across this part of the desert before, but I'm sure we're not likely to find a spring anywhere in the direction we'll be going."

"Well, this was the best the trainmen could come up with, so I guess we'll just have to make do with it," Tim said. "But it sounds to me like you expect us to have a long way to go."

"Wouldn't you say Ki's right, Da?" Nora put in. "Don't forget the horses will need water as much as we do. And remember how tiny the bag looked the last time we saw it? We're likely to have a long trip before we find it."

"I'm not arguing, lass," Tim replied. "From the look of this country, I misdoubt we'll find a spring or pond where we can get more water if we need it."

Ki had been taking a final look at the loaded wagon during the exchange between Tim and Nora. He turned to them now and said, "We're as ready as we'll ever be. Let's start out."

Swinging into Sun's saddle while Nora and Tim climbed onto the wagon seat, Ki turned the palomino's head south and nudged its belly softly with his sandaled toe. Ahead, the tan-colored soil of the desert stretched to a horizon that seemed to be infinitely distant. Only an occasional clump of ground-hugging cactus and the even rarer cylinder of a towering saguaro broke the land between them and the level line where the tan earth ended and the cloudless sky began. Sun moved forward and the wagon creaked as it started to follow.

Jessie needed only one glance at the horsemen and their rifles and gunbelts to realize that any effort to resist them would be futile. She let her Colt drop to the ground and raised her hands. When Ted saw Jessie's arms go up, he lifted his as well. They stood silently, gazing at the riders, who in turn were watching them with undisguised curiosity.

Almost to a man, the outlaws wore the loose, thin cotton trousers and jackets that were common to field workers, ranch hands, and other laborers along the border. Their faces revealed their Indian-Spanish blood, for their mustaches grew thick and black while their unshaven cheeks either had a thin straggle of beard or were hairless, and their chins were universally bare.

There were a few who did not wear straw hats, but had on tapering high-crowned felt hats with brims dished upward like small bowls. The hat worn by the one who was obviously the leader bore an elaborate pattern of entwined gold threads on its crown. All of them carried rifles and had on gunbelts supporting a holstered revolver. Two or three sported cartridge bandoliers over a shoulder, and the leader wore a pair of bandoliers crossed over his chest.

Their faces were what had come to be called in Mexico *"tipo Benito"*, in tribute to the peasant leader Juárez: square-jawed, with full lips, thick fleshy noses, and high cheekbones, their deepset eyes as black as obsidian and as impenetrable.

Without taking his eyes off Jessie and Ted, the leader of the band snapped out a quick command in Spanish. One of the riders behind him dismounted and walked toward them, not bothering to draw his revolver.

Both the leader and his men had shifted their rifles into the crooks of their elbows. Jessie knew that the weapons could be brought to bear in a split second. The man moving toward them circled Jessie, bent down briefly to pick up her Colt and tuck it into his waistband, then walked to the basket and gestured for Ted to get out.

Ted vaulted over the rim and dropped lightly to his feet, raising his arms again at once. The man flicked his eyes over the balloonist before moving to the basket and pulling himself up by the basket rim to glance inside it.

"No hay ningún de valor, Chaco," he called to the leader. *"Ni armas, ni dinero, no ropas, solamente un cordela y algunas latas. Que quieres hace ahora?"*

"Traeles aqui," the man addressed as Chaco replied. He turned to the horsemen behind him and ran his eyes over them, then went on, pointing as he spoke, *"Escueleto! Y tu también, Niguto, quedarse y velartese el globo. Llevarnos estes gringos al abrigo."*

"De qual tiempo, Chaco?" the man addressed as Niguto asked. *"No hay agua, no hay alimentos."*

"No es importante!" Chaco snapped. *"Hace que dicho!"*

As the two men he'd indicated began moving slowly toward the balloon, the one who'd come forward first stepped behind Jessie and Ted.

"Andale," he commanded, prodding each of them in turn with the muzzle of Jessie's Colt. *"Y cuidado. No mi importa un bledo a matales!"*

Neither of them needed a translation of the harsh command and its threat. They started walking slowly forward.

"Did you understand what they were saying?" Ted whispered.

"Don't let on," she replied, keeping her voice as low as his. "I know a little Spanish, but I don't want them to realize that I do. The man behind us told the leader there wasn't anything valuable in the balloon, and what he just said was that it wouldn't bother him to kill us if we didn't obey him. The leader sent those men coming toward us to guard the balloon, so I guess he intends to take us somewhere else. Their camp, I imagine."

Forgetting to whisper, Ted began, "But we didn't see—"

"Callate!" their guard barked, emphasizing what he'd said by prodding Ted painfully with the revolver.

Jessie and Ted did not try to speak again as they covered the short distance to the leader. They stopped in front of his horse and stood silently while he looked at them closely. For almost a full minute the man they'd heard called Chaco shifted his eyes from Jessie to Ted and back to Jessie. At last he spoke.

"What for you are here, gringos?"

Jessie glanced quickly at Ted, who shrugged and nodded that he expected her to be their spokesman.

"We're here because this is where the wind carried our balloon," she replied. "Nobody sent us, if that's what you want to know."

"From where you have come?"

"New Mexico," Jessie answered promptly. "A place called Silver City."

From the unchanged expression on Chaco's face, Jessie could not tell whether or not he understood her. For a moment he stared at her and Ted, then turned his attention to the balloon again. At last he looked back at them.

"Is worth *mucho dinero,* this thing?" he asked.

Jessie pretended not to understand. He repeated his question, this time pointing to the balloon. Jessie shrugged and asked. "How much is a horse worth to a man who can't ride it?"

"Oho! You are a smart *gringa!*" Chaco grinned, his lips parting to show big, yellowed teeth with a gap in his lower jaw where an eyetooth was missing. "You think I am *cholo estúpido,* no? You think I am not see *globo* before now?" When he paused and Jessie did not reply, his thick black eyebrows pulled into a frown and he went on, "I am see *globo* go in air, I know what is do. Now, you tell me what I ask you, no? How many *dólares de Estados Unidos* is worth?"

"Right now it's not even worth one of your *centavos,*" Jessie replied coolly. "As long as it stays on the ground, it's just a lot of cloth. This man standing by me is the only one who knows how to make it go up in the air."

For a moment, Chaco's frown returned as he thought over Jessie's reply. Then he nodded slowly and said, *"Es verdad."* Turning to Ted, he asked, "How long it takes to learn this thing, to make *el globo* go up?"

Ted glanced at Jessie for a clue. She raised her eyebrows and shook her head in an almost imperceptible movement. Ted kept his eyes on her for a moment, then turned back to the bandit leader.

"If you're smart, you might learn in two or three years," he said. Then, as Chaco began to smile, he added quickly, "If you can keep from falling and killing yourself."

Chaco's smile turned into a frown. He asked. "How you are stop it from fall?"

"That's what it takes two or three years to learn," Ted replied calmly.

110

After a long moment of thoughtful silence, Chaco repeated the question he'd already asked Jessie. "How much is worth, *el globo?*"

Now it was Ted's turn to be silent. When several minutes had ticked away without Chaco getting an answer to his question, Jessie saw that the bandit was growing impatient and tried to change the subject.

"Listen to me, Chaco," she said. "The balloon's not worth anything to you. It's not worth anything to us, either, as long as we can't use it. Now, name a price for letting us go."

"And how you will pay me, if I do this?" the bandit asked mockingly. "You 'ave no money."

Jessie realized too late that she'd been underestimating Chaco, and tried to correct the mistake as best she could. She said quickly, "I can get money, if you'll take us to the nearest town where there's a telegraph office."

"Ah." Chaco nodded, a mocking smile forming on his face. "So I do this thing you say, and who you are send *telégrafo* for to get this money, they will tell *los rurales,* then *los rurales* they wait where this money is deliver, and we will fight."

"No!" Jessie protested, with a sinking feeling that she was fighting a losing battle. "I will tell them not to call in the *rurales!* Believe me, Chaco, I'll be fair with you!"

"De verdad," the bandid sneered. "Was never time when *guachapine* is fair with *peon!* I am no fool, *gringa!* Better I am keep you until me and my men we get tired of you, then I am take you to Chihuahua, and sell you for *puta.* This way, I am have no trouble!"

Jessie knew that Chaco was deadly serious. She understood how cheap life was in Mexico, realized that the *rurales* were brutally merciless, and that women were sold into prostitution. She knew also that from his point of view

111

the bandit was not being cold-blooded, but practical, and she had no doubt at all that he'd do just as he'd threatened.

"I'm telling you the truth," she said, determined to make a last effort, even if it was useless. "I have friends in many places across the border. They will be glad to help me."

"Bah!" Chaco snorted. "Me and my men have no friends, so we will help ourselves." Without taking his eyes off Jessie and Ted, he called, "Escueleto! Nigua!" As the two men stepped forward, Chaco snapped, *"Guardes el globo hasta volveremos!"*

Turning to the rest of his followers, the outlaw leader pointed to one, and jerked his thumb toward Ted. He gestured to another to boost Jessie up on his saddle behind him. The outlaws jumped to obey, and hurried to remount. With a last glance around, Chaco waved toward the west, and the little group rode off.

In the desert country they crossed, there were no landmarks to give Jessie a sure way to judge distance. She knew only that they had been riding for a long time and the sun was dipping close to the horizon when she saw the massive butte rising on the flat horizon. Thrusting up from a featureless landscape, the huge, humped formation was all that broke the straight line where sky met earth as far as her eyes could see.

Before they reached the butte the sun had dropped even lower and they rode in its shadow until they reached the base and moved beside the towering wall of stone. Suddenly the riders in front seemed to disappear. Jessie hid her surprise when the man in the saddle reined the horse into a dark cleft that split the cliff from top to base. The slit was barely wide enough for a man on horseback to pass through, then suddenly it ended and they emerged into a box canyon.

Jessie had not been prepared for everything that met her eyes as they adjusted to its interior shade. The open space before her was large enough to contain a small village instead of the three ramshackle huts spaced well apart that stood along one side of the oval-shaped enclosure. A tiny spring bubbling from the wall in the back formed a trickling brook only two or three handspans wide that cut across the oval floor and disappeared below the opposite wall. There a thin thread of smoke rose from a crude fire pit circled with boulders. Blanket rolls and boxes were scattered on the ground around the fire pit.

Chaco swung out of his saddle, and gestured to the men who carried Jessie and Ted. The riders toed their horses close to one of the huts and unceremoniously shoved their passengers to the ground.

"Andales al jacal," one of them said harshly, jerking his thumb toward the open door.

There was no way Jessie and Ted could pretend that they did not understand this command. Without protesting, they went into the hut, Jessie could tell at a glance that the shanty was very old indeed. It had been made from saplings bound together by rawhide strips intertwined among the trunks. Between the wrist-thick saplings, the bindings created wide cracks through which they could see the outlaws moving about, settling down.

Jessie wondered why the shanties had been constructed in the first place, for they were floorless and roofless. After a few seconds of speculation while she and Ted glanced around the interior of their prison and found it totally barren, both of them began peering through the cracks to observe the activities of their captors.

113

"They don't seem to be at all concerned about us," Ted said as they watched. "They didn't even put a guard at the door."

"Why should they?" Jessie managed a small wry smile. "How much chance would we have of getting away?"

"None, I suppose," Ted admitted. "And I'd give a lot to know why they even bothered to bring us here."

"I'm sure the balloon was the reason. Chaco's a very ruthless outlaw, but he's shrewd. My guess is that he's trying to think of a way to get a lot of money fast by using it."

"How, Jessie?"

"I don't know, and I'll bet he doesn't either. He knows how much I'd be worth if he carried out his threat to sell me, but if it won't bother you to be reminded of it, you're not a salable piece of merchandise. Chaco's keeping you alive to teach him how to handle the balloon."

A worried frown had passed over Ted's face as Jessie spoke, but he shook his head and managed a grim smile before saying, "I'll see him rot in hell before I teach him, Jessie."

"Don't be too sure, Ted. Getting slivers of wood stuck under your fingernails and lighted has made a lot of very strong men change their minds."

"That doesn't sound very pleasant, and I'm sure it's a lot worse than it sounds. But I simply can't think of any possible use the balloon could be to a bandit."

"Oh, I can," Jessie said slowly. "Sending up a balloon a quarter of a mile outside a medium-sized Mexican town would empty the streets and shops very fast. A few men could do a lot of looting in a short time if there wasn't anybody to stop them."

"I hadn't thought of that."

"I'm not sure Chaco has, either, but I'm afraid he will."

114

"What are we going to do, then?"

"Nothing, until dark. Then we'll have to try to get away." Jessie looked at the bare floor. "This might not be a very comfortable place to sleep, but I'm going to try to have a nap."

She stretched out on the hard dirt and in a very few minutes was sleeping soundly, her head resting on her outstretched arm.

Fingers brushing across her cheek brought Jessie wide-awake. The hut was in darkness except for the few dim rays of orange-hued light that trickled through the cracks in one wall.

"What's wrong, Ted?" Jessie asked, her voice just a bit louder than a whisper. She could see her companion only as a black outline against the hut's wall. "Is something happening?"

"No. The outlaws seem to be going to bed, all except one who's standing guard at the opening."

"Apparently Chaco's decided to let us go hungry. I'm not surprised. He's shrewd enough to know that starving us is one of the best ways to break down our resistance."

"Are you hungry?"

"Of course. Aren't you?"

"I think I'm more worried than I am hungry," Ted replied. "I can't understand why they don't pay any attention to us."

Thinking of the times she'd been held captive during her battles with the cartel, Jessie said, "Isolating us goes with starving us. They might not come near us for two or three days."

"You sound like you've had some experience at this."

"I have, a little. What about you?"

"No. Being a prisoner's something new. And sort of

115

surprising, too." Ted hesitated before going on, then said, "I was sitting here watching you sleep before it got too dark to see you, and I couldn't think of anything but how beautiful you are. I forgot about everything else."

"I appreciate your thoughts, Ted," Jessie said. "But this is a strange place for them to occur to you."

"Not any stranger than the basket of the balloon when the levanter was blowing us here. Or when I took you up for the first time, back on your ranch."

"And you've never said anything until now?"

"No. I—well, if you want the truth, Jessie, I'm sort of tongue-tied where some women are concerned. I always have been. Some—not at all. You're one of them, of course."

"Now, I can't understand that. You're an attractive man."

"Attractive to you?"

"Yes, certainly. But I thought perhaps you and Nora—"

Ted broke in, "No. Not Nora. She's like a sister to me."

Their odd conversation in such an unlikely place was having its effect on Jessie. She was silent for a moment, thinking of the unpredictable future and the unstable present. Then she whispered, "Ted, why don't you do more than just think about me?"

Jessie was unprepared for the eager response that followed her suggestion. Ted swept her up into his arms, and in spite of his professed shyness found her lips with his in a fraction of a second. She felt the top of his tongue probing after they'd held their kiss for several moments, and opened her lips to meet it with hers.

Ted began caressing her with his big, strong hands, stroking the globes of her breasts, and when Jessie let one of her hands fall to his thigh she felt the swelling of his erection. Without breaking their kiss, she twisted slightly to reach her blouse and unbutton it, then gave her attention to freeing the thickening cylinder of flesh that now bulged below Ted's trousers.

By now Ted had helped Jessie shrug her blouse off her shoulders and his lips were slipping down to find the budded tips of her taut, full breasts. Jessie stepped out of the low-cut boots she'd chosen to wear in the balloon, and pulled up her skirt to slide off her pantalettes.

Ted's lips were exploring the sensitive tips of her breasts now and when Jessie once more took him into her hand she found him engorged and fully erect. Leaning toward him, she whispered, "I'm ready for you now, Ted. Whenever you—"

Ted needed no further invitation. He moved above her and waited while she placed him, then drove in. Jessie gasped as he sank into her, and rose to meet him when he began thrusting. After her long period of abstinence at the Circle Star, Jessie's response was as quick as his.

She did not count the moments, for time is of little account on such occasions, but as Ted gasped and thrust with a final expiratory lunge her own climax took her, and with a gusty cry and a long, wavering sigh she quivered through her culmination. Ted had already fallen forward limp when her body at last stopped quaking and she lay still.

Jessie listened and, when she realized that there was silence outside as well as within the little shanty, she lifted her lips to Ted's ear and whispered, "We don't have to move, Ted. The bandits have all gone to sleep. As long as we don't disturb them, we've got the rest of the night for ourselves."

Chapter 11

"Ki, I sure as hell hope you've got some idea where we're heading for," Tim O'Brien said as the wagon thumped and lurched across the stony bed of a dry wash.

Since they'd started from the railroad the day before, the wide, shallow gully bottomed with loose rocks was the first sign they'd come across so far that even hinted that at some long-ago time water had flowed across the arid land. The wagon reached level land at the edge of the wash and Tim reined in to let the horse breathe. Ki reined Sun in and stopped beside the wagon.

"I hope I do, Tim," he replied soberly. "I'm doing the only thing that occurs to me."

"There's one thing about this country," Nora said. "We can see for a long way in every direction. There's no danger of missing the balloon even if we're five or ten miles off course."

"Which we might well be," Ki told her. "But we know that we're going in the direction where we saw the balloon going down, and even as deserted as this country is, we're sure to run across somebody sooner or later. A balloon isn't something they'd see every day, so they'd certainly have noticed it and could tell us which way it was moving."

"We've been traveling steadily since yesterday after-

118

noon, and haven't seen anybody yet," Nora said. "And there's nothing ahead of us that I can see. It's the most deserted place I've ever been in."

"That's what makes it seem like we've been traveling longer than we really have," Ki observed. "But we knew when we started that it wasn't going to be an easy trip."

Touching Sun's flank with his toe, Ki started the palomino walking again. Tim slapped the reins over the back of the wagon horse and followed. Ahead of them the desert stretched flat until it met the horizon. With the setting sun to their sides, they moved on across the barren, featureless land. The only sounds that broke the stillness were the clopping of the horses' hooves on the barren soil and the creaking of the wagon.

Ki did not call a halt until the afterglow of sunset was beginning to fade to a thin strip of bluish-red hanging above a perfectly level horizon. He reined Sun in and swept his eyes from side to side, then turned to the others.

"This is as good a place as any for us to stop," he told them. "It's too bad there's no moon, or we might push on a few more miles."

"I'm certainly ready to call it a day," Nora said. "And even if Da denies it, he's getting tired of jolting in this wagon seat." She turned to Tim and said, "You must be stiff and sore by now, Da. You'd better make your bed in the wagon tonight, and I'll sleep on the ground."

"Now, don't go trying to make an old lady out of me," Tim told her. "You've heard me say it before, it's a man's place to sleep on the ground and let ladies be comfortable in the wagon."

Nora and Ki exchanged glances. Tim's insistence that she sleep in the wagon had kept them apart since leaving Silver City. Even there they'd managed only two nights together in the hotel.

"All right," Nora said resignedly. "Be stubborn, for all I care. Now, we'd better get our bedrolls spread and have a bite of supper. It's going to be too dark to see by the time we finish eating."

It was the dark of the moon, and night had already settled down when they finished their pickup meal, though there was still a faint afterglow above the horizon to the west. They'd pulled the dunnage boxes into the center of the wagonbed to sit on while eating summer sausage and cheese and crackers from the provisions bought at the railroad commissary, and Ki helped Tim push the boxes to the sides to give Nora room to spread her bedroll. As Ki stepped over the wagon seat, Tim called to him.

"Would you give me a hand over the seat, Ki? This stick I've got for a leg don't bend as good as me real one does."

Ki stood up on the seat to pull Tim up, and waited there for the old Irishman to maneuver his wooden leg in getting out of the wagon. Tim walked away and vanished in the gloom, and Ki understood that the old balloonist was going aside to relieve himself.

Ki started to step off the wagon seat and follow Tim to the ground when a sudden flicker of reddish light on the darkening horizon caught his eyes. The tiny dot twinkled for a few seconds and then disappeared as suddenly as it had popped out. Ki stood motionless, his gaze fixed on the spot where he'd seen the almost unnoticeable pinpoint, but it did not recur.

"Is something wrong, Ki?" Nora asked.

"I'm not sure there's anything wrong," Ki said, frowning. "But I'm sure I saw something flare up somewhere ahead of us."

"I didn't see anything," she said.

"You wouldn't, from where you're standing. Up here on the seat my eyes are a couple of feet higher than yours."

120

"Meaning there's somebody not too far away?"

"Seven miles or less, Nora. That's how far a man on a horse can see in flat country like this, and my eyes are just about at the level where they'd be if I was in the saddle."

"You're sure you didn't just see a low-hanging star?"

Ki shook his head. "It was just a pinpoint of light, but I could tell it was something like a match flare. Stars are clear white, but the light I saw was sort of red or orange."

"Do you think it could be Ted and Jessie?"

"That's the first thing I thought of. Then I realized the only reason they'd have for striking a match would be to light a fire or a lantern, and I'd have seen more light if that had been the reason for the match."

"If it was a match you saw, what other reason would somebody have for striking it?"

"To light a cigar or cigarette," Ki said thoughtfully. "Or to look for something, but if they'd been doing anything like that the light would've lasted longer, and if it really was somebody lighting a cigar or cigarette, it wouldn't be Jessie or Ted."

"No, it wouldn't," Nora agreed. She was silent for a moment, then asked, "What're you going to do, Ki? Go look for whoever it is?"

"Not tonight. That would be like looking for the needle in the haystack. But I'll ride ahead of the wagon in the—" Ki broke off and shook his head. "No. You and Tim stay here in the morning. I'll get up early and go investigate. Mexico's not a peaceful place to be in right now, Nora, especially this close to the border."

"Do you want us to follow you later, then?"

"No. I'll double back as soon—" Ki broke off as he heard Tim's footsteps returning. "When you wake up in the morning, explain to your father where I've gone and why."

• • •

121

Having gone through the rigid mental discipline required to become a master of the Oriental martial arts, Ki had the ability to sleep for a self-chosen period of time. He woke, instantly alert, sat up in his bedroll and glanced at the eastern sky. He could see the line of the horizon in the false dawn, and could dimly make out the outline of Tim's bedroll next to his, and the legs of the horses tethered to the wagon tongue, but only as vague shadows lacking detail.

Getting up quickly and moving silently, Ki saddled Sun and led him away from the wagon until he felt it was safe to swing into the saddle and ride. Once in the saddle, he set his course by the line of darkness to the west, where the western horizon cut off the stars. Except for the grating of Sun's hooves on the baked soil, the morning was quiet in the before-dawn stillness.

In this harsh semidesert country, lizards and snakes were the only wildlife, and occasionally a tiny, almost inaudible scratching on the hard soil told Ki that a lizard had just scuttled out of his path, but aside from the thunking of Sun's hooves, that was the only noise he heard. Now and then he looked back at the slowly brightening eastern sky. A well-defined line now marked the horizon, and he could see the rectangular shape of the wagon directly behind him, so diminished in size now as to look like a child's toy, but still quite visible and identifiable.

In front of him the land was still shrouded in darkness. Behind him, while the sun's rim still remained below the horizon, its rays were brightening an increasingly large arc of the eastern sky. The spot Ki had marked in his memory last night was directly across from the bright center of the arc, and a thoughtful frown formed on his face as he debated the equations posed by the factors of time and distance. When he was sure he'd solved the mental equation, he reined Sun to the north, still keeping up his slow, steady pace. When he'd covered a mile or so he changed directions again; now he was advancing at right angles to his last course.

While his zigzag moves had increased the distance Ki still had to cover to reach the spot he'd targeted the night before, the movements had changed the angle of his approach. They had also delayed by a few minutes the time when the rising sun would be directly at his back, silhouetting him against the brightest area of the sky when its rim broke over the horizon. The new angle would also give him a better perspective of the spot that was his goal.

Ki did not alter the steady pace at which he'd been moving, though in spite of his training a part of his mind was urging him to go faster. Another quarter hour passed before his patience was rewarded. The light grew steadily brighter in the area that was his goal, and as the visibility increased he saw what he'd not yet allowed himself to admit he'd been hoping to find: the balloon's boxlike basket draped in the shimmering, wrinkled fabric of the big bag itself.

Reining in without delay, Ki slid from the saddle. Only the bottom of the basket was visible now beneath the folds of the bag. He patted the palomino's neck and said, "Stand, Sun!" Then he began trotting at a steady pace toward the deflated balloon.

Ki kept his eyes fixed on his goal as his ground-eating trot brought him closer to the balloon. He saw the man rounding the corner of the basket in time to drop flat. He hugged the ground for a moment, not sure that he'd escaped being seen, but as the moments passed and he heard no shout, no footsteps running toward him, Ki raised his head and saw that the man had backed away from the basket and was standing facing it, staring at the crumpled folds of the bag.

Ki resumed his advance, trotting faster than before. When the man beside the balloon started moving again, he dropped flat at once and raised his head carefully until the man was once more visible. He'd started toward the basket again now, and he stopped when he reached it. Then the man began pawing at the balloon's fabric, trying to lift it off the basket.

When Ki started forward once more he no longer felt it was necessary to crawl. He got to his feet and ran, bent over, ready to drop flat the instant the figure beside the basket gave any sign of turning around. He could see the man very clearly now, for the sky was brightening rapidly. Though the wide-brimmed sombrero he was wearing kept his face in deep shadow, Ki noted that he had a revolver belted at his waist.

Although Ki was very close to the balloon now, he knew that he could not get near enough to throw a *shuriken* with the pinpoint accuracy that the situation required, nor could he win a race to close the distance before his quarry cut him down with a bullet from the revolver. He stopped his advance and flattened out on the ground again to watch and wait.

When he saw the man fish a sack of tobacco from his pocket and begin rolling a cigarette, Ki took the opportunity to gain a few more yards, but was forced to stop and flatten out prone again when his quarry turned toward him, licked the seam of his cigarette, and lighted it. Then Ki started forward once more when he saw the man turn his back, bend down, and try once again to lift the fabric of the bag.

Ki was on the verge of resuming his stealthy advance when the man beside the balloon suddenly abandoned his efforts and raised his voice to call, *"Nigua! Vente 'ca y ayudami!"*

A second man, his clothing almost duplicating that of

124

the first, came from behind the basket. He was stretching as he walked and the gruffness of sleep was still in his voice as he asked, *"Qué tal, Escueleto?"*

"Ayudami elevé el globo."

"Porque?"

"Tal vez es algún de valor ahí."

"Cagado, hombre! No es algún aya! Esto vemos ayer!"

"Hace que dijo!" Escueleto snapped angrily, grabbing his companion's arm.

Nigua pulled his arm from Escueleto's grasp and pushed him away. Escueleto kicked his companion in the shins, and Nigua yelled angrily. The two men grappled, swaying.

Ki had spent enough time along the Texas-Mexico border and in Mexico itself to have recognized the pair as outlaws by now. Though his command of Spanish was limited, he'd picked up enough of the language from Mexican cowpokes to understand their argument. He saw his opportunity and took it.

By now the two men had broken their close hold and were swaying with arms intertwined, trying to throw one another. Ki leaped to his feet, sliding a pair of *shuriken* from the pocket of his vest. He aimed one at the man called Escueleto and let it fly, then immediately slid the second *shuriken* into his right hand and sailed it toward Nigua.

He'd aimed low, intending to sink the razor-toothed blades into their chests and put them out of action, but even as Ki launched the wicked toothed blades the scuffling pair shifted positions. Ki's first *shuriken* slashed into Nigua's neck just below the jawbone and severed the outlaw's ropelike sternal muscle, then pierced the carotid artery below it, bringing a jet of blood gushing forth. The second blade dug into one side of Escueleto's chest and struck just above his right armpit, lodging in his pectoral muscle.

Both men reeled and parted as the whirling blades bit

into their flesh. Nigua dropped to the ground, clawing at his throat from which his lifeblood was draining in great pulsing spurts. Escueleto did not fall, but staggered, bending doubled over, one hand going up to grab at the *shuriken* embedded in his chest, trying to bring up his other hand to reach his gun butt.

Ki was running toward the two outlaws by now, a fresh blade in each hand. Nigua was sprawled on the ground, a gurgling noise coming from his split throat. Escueleto was still trying to raise his right hand high enough to grasp the butt of his pistol, but the pain of moving his arm kept him from drawing the weapon in a single sweep.

Ki reached him just as the pistol cleared its holster, and he whirled in a *mae-geri* kick that sent the weapon sailing away. The kick also jarred the man's arm and increased the pain of the embedded *shuriken*. He yowled and sagged to the ground beside Nigua, whose gasping sighs were fading as his life ebbed away. Ki planted a foot on Escueleto's left hand and stood looking down at the outlaw's pain-twisted face.

For a moment the silence was broken only by the groans of the wounded outlaw. Then the man looked up at Ki, his eyes wide with a mixture of perplexity and fear. When Ki said nothing, but returned the stare with a menacing frown, Escueleto twisted his head, searching for his companion. He saw the sprawled corpse lying a few feet away and looked back at Ki, moaning as his movement intensified the pain of the *shuriken* that was still. embedded in his chest.

"Nigua, el es muerto," he gasped.

Ki nodded and said coldly, "You'll be as dead as he is if you don't tell me what I want to know." He was watching the outlaw's face as he spoke and saw his eyelids flicker. Taking the almost imperceptible move as a sign that his captive understood English, Ki kept his voice harsh and threatening as he asked, "Where are the man and woman from the balloon?"

Escueleto looked up, his face twisted in pain. When he saw the *shuriken* Ki was holding poised he shook his head and raised his hand in a silent plea for mercy before answering, *"Al hoyo, Chaco tomelos ahí."*

"Chaco?" Ki asked. "Who's he?"

"Chaco es mi jefe," the outlaw replied.

"Speak English!" Ki snapped. "I know you can understand it, so you can speak it, too! Is Chaco your boss?"

Escueleto's jaw tightened, but he nodded, then said, *"Sí.* Is what you say, boss."

"Then tell me where this Chaco took the man and the woman."

"El hoyo," Escueleto gasped. He tried to lift his free arm to point, but the pain of moving started his body quivering. He groaned and let his arm fall, then went on. *"El hoyo es—"*

"I told you to speak English!" Ki repeated harshly.

"Hoyo is hole. Hole in little hill."

"A cave?"

"Is not cave. Is go up from ground to top of hill."

"A hole in a hill?" Ki frowned. "You mean a box canyon?"

"Sí." Escueleto nodded eagerly, then grimaced as his move brought on another surge of pain. "Box *cañón."*

"Which way is this canyon?"

"Al oeste, west, like you say."

"How far west is it?"

"Six, seven *millas,* maybe."

"Directly to the west?"

Again Escueleto tired to shrug and grimaced in pain. Then he said, "Is west. Is all I can say. You will see it, is not big hill, but no place you look, is no more hill."

Ki nodded. "All right, I guess you've done the best you can." He looked at the *shuriken*, still buried in the outlaw's chest, and went on, "Now, I'm going to pull that blade out and bandage you up."

Excueleto's eyes opened wide. "You are not to kill me?"

"No. Not if I find that hill you told me about. But if you've been lying to me—"

"Is not lie!" the outlaw broke in. "Is hill, is *hoyo*, where I say!"

"If it's there, I'll find it," Ki promised. "Now let's see what I can do to fix your shoulder."

Chapter 12

"Do you think they're ever going to feed us, Jessie?" Ted asked. "I don't know how long it's been since sunup, but those men have been stirring around ever since it got light enough for us to see anything down in this hole."

"Sooner or later," Jessie replied, "they'll certainly give us enough food to keep us alive."

They were standing side by side at the wall of their prison shanty, watching the outlaws through the cracks between the saplings. The morning sunshine was just beginning to creep into the box canyon, forming a bright crescent on the rim of the high stone wall across from their prison. The outlaws were hunkered down around a small fire near the outlet of the creek, using folded tortillas to scoop up food from an iron pot that stood at the edge of the flickering blaze.

"They act like they've forgotten we're here," Ted said, and frowned.

"They haven't. Don't worry about that. Latins can be almost as patient and devious as Orientals when it serves their purpose."

"If I understand what you're saying, they're trying to make us nervous by ignoring us."

"Of course they are, Ted! And remember, when people

129

are hungry it's a lot easier to persuade them to talk."

"I'm hungry right now, but I'd have to be a lot hungrier to change my mind about teaching that Chaco fellow to handle the balloon."

"Just be prepared for him to threaten you, too," Jessie warned her companion. "He's almost certain to use a threat of torture as well as starvation to remind us what they can do if they want to."

Ted looked at Jessie, a small frown wrinkling his brow. "From what you've been saying, I get the idea you've been a prisoner before, Jessie. At least you seem to know a lot about it."

"My father had some very unscrupulous business enemies," she replied. "They captured me a time or two and tried to use me as a threat to make Alex give in to their demands."

"And he never did?"

"No. Alex and Ki always managed to find me and get me out of danger."

"That explains why you're being so calm about this, then." Ted nodded. "But are you sure that Ki's going to be able to find us this time? Remember, he hasn't any idea where we are."

"If I know Ki, he's been following us ever since that wild wind caught us. And Ki doesn't give up easily, Ted."

"You really think he could follow us at the speed we were moving?"

"We were high enough to be visible for a long time. I'm sure he managed somehow."

"And you think he can get us away from that gang out there, with only Tim and Nora to help him?"

"I have a feeling that he will," Jessie said. "Don't underestimate Ki. He has his own way of fighting."

• • •

At the time when Jessie and Ted were discussing him, Ki was sitting in the wagon having a late lunch with Nora and Tim while he told the new arrivals what he'd learned from Escueleto. Tim and Nora had reached the balloon only a short time earlier, the wagon horse lathered and panting after its forced run following the trail of hoofprints left earlier in the day by Sun.

"But do you think you can believe what that outlaw told you?" Nora asked, glancing at Escueleto, lying on the bare ground a few yards away, his wrists and ankles bound.

"He wasn't lying to me, Nora," Ki assured her. "I'd take him with me, but he's too badly hurt to travel. Anyhow, he'd just hinder me."

"You're going to take on that gang by yourself, Ki?" Nora frowned.

"There are only a half-dozen of them left. When I find the place he described, I don't think I'll have too much trouble getting Jessie and Ted free."

Tim joined the discussion, saying, "Ki knows what he's doing, girl, and we'd best let him do it his way. Besides, after he's gone we'll be getting onto our own job. While we're keeping an eye on that fellow over yonder, we'll have to be neatening up the bag and folding it to go on the wagon. You know how long that'll take."

"I should, Da. I've helped you and Ted do it enough times."

"Well, then," Tim went on. "If all of us know what we're to do, hadn't we better be going at it?"

Glancing at the sun, just past its zenith, Ki said, "If Escueleto wasn't lying to me about the distance to the outlaw's roost, I'll have just enough time to get there with plenty of daylight left to scout out the ground."

"When will you be back, then?" Nora asked.

"Before this time tomorrow at the latest. The exact time

131

will depend on too many things I can't plan for until I see the place where the gang's holding them."

"We'll be waiting," she assured him. "And good luck, Ki."

Ki nodded as he stepped down from the wagon. He walked over to Sun, swung into the saddle, and rode off.

To keep Sun as fresh as possible, Ki did not push the big palomino. He let the horse set its own pace, touching the reins only occasionally. Even if Escueleto had not given him directions he'd have had little difficulty following the outlaw gang to its hideout. His sharp eyes flicking over the barren desert soil saw many indications of the route the bandits had followed, as well as revealing that there were five men in the outlaw gang.

As hard as the sunbaked desert soil was, its crust held the shallow imprints of horseshoes, and to a tracker of Ki's skill, each shoe told its own story. One of the horses was shod with shoes that had both toe and heel caulks, one had only toe caulks and a third had only heel caulks. Of the two that had no caulks at all, one horse had wide, rounded hooves, the other's hooves were elongated, more oval in shape. Two sets of the hoofprints were deeper and much more clearly marked than the others, and this was enough to tell Ki that they were carrying a double load, Jessie on one horse, Ted on the other.

In addition to the information Ki read in the hoofprints, there were other signs on the ground. He saw horse droppings, still glistening fresh; butts of cornhusk cigarettes; and on the rare stretches where the soil was soft enough, the hoofprints had the clean, sharp outlines that showed them to be only a few hours old. Even if Ki had not known the direction in which the outlaw hideout lay, he would have had no trouble in following the outlaws' tracks to it.

Dusk was only a short time away when Ki spotted the

humped formation through which the box canyon rose. It stood alone in the otherwise featureless vista, a cone-shaped mesa that must once have been the crest of some long-dead volcano, eroded now, jutting above the expanse of sunbaked soil like a thumb that had been severed from the hand of a unimaginably monstrous giant.

Reining in, Ki studied the landscape for a moment. He saw no movement, no distinguishing landmarks, and toed Sun forward, reining the horse to ride on a long diagonal toward his goal. As he drew closer, Ki touched the reins only when he wanted Sun to follow the course he'd picked while he was studying the mesa, a wide semicircle. He was looking for the slit Escueleto had described to him, the eroded vent or chimney of the extinct volcano that gave access to the box canyon inside it.

As soon as he saw the slit, a black crack that ran from the crown of the mesa to its base, Ki could tell even at a distance that one or two men could hold off a thousand from its shelter. The barren desert stretched away from the slit without even a hump or crevasse on the ground that would provide cover for anyone trying to enter the box canyon.

His need for detail satisfied, Ki turned Sun and rode at a slant toward the mesa's blind wall a short distance from the slit. Though he knew from experience that Sun would stand until doomsday when commanded to do so, Ki rode around the base of the mesa until he found another opening in its erosion-seamed face.

He did not have far to look. He saw a narrow cut in the wall only a short distance from the first opening. It was shallow, but deep enough to shield the palomino from being noticed with a passing glance. He backed Sun into the crevice, found a stone heavy to weight down the reins, then sat down at its mouth. Leaning back against the towering wall, Ki waited with Oriental patience for the declining sun to drop still lower before making his foray.

Inside the box canyon, Jessie and Ted were growing hungrier by the minute. They were standing at the shanty wall, watching the outlaws through its cracks. Ted's arm was around Jessie's waist, pressing her to him. While their long night together had welded them as lovers, they'd faced reality at daybreak and had agreed that their captors must get no hint of their changed relationship.

However, as the day dragged on the outlaws had continued to ignore them. Though now and then one or another of the bandits had glanced at the shanty while passing it, they'd had no other attention. It was as though the outlaws had agreed to forget or ignore their presence.

"I still wish they'd give us something to eat," Ted said as he watched the activity on the canyon floor.

Three of the gang were sitting by the still-smoking coals of the fire that they'd rekindled at noon to warm the pot from which all of them ate. Two were squatting against the wall mending harnesses, and Chaco himself was standing in the gap that led outside.

Once she'd noticed the sunlight crawling slowly down the canyon's inner wall, Jessie had realized that by glancing at it now and then she could fix the approximate time of day. She'd watched the wall brighten through the morning until at noon the sun bathed the center of the canyon floor. Now the floor was in the sort of subdued light that outside would be seen only during a brief period after sunset, and the line of sunshine had risen more than halfway up the eastern wall.

"In a little while they'll be heating up whatever's in that pot for supper," Jessie said encouragingly. "Surely they'll feed us before they go to bed."

"Maybe they're planning on starving us until I agree to show them how to reinflate the balloon," Ted suggested. "That Chaco fellow was really interested in it."

Jessie saw the logic of his suggestion at once. "Starving us into submission is the kind of thing they'd be likely to try," she agreed. "But I'm sure Ki will find us before we get very hungry."

"I'm what I'd call very hungry right now," Ted told her. "But I've been that way before, so I'm not complaining."

"They might just be waiting until it's dark," Jessie suggested. "Though I can't see why they should feel they have to take that precaution in this sheltered place. But whatever's going to happen, all we can do is wait and take it as it comes."

Ki woke from the light sleep he'd fallen into and glanced at the shadow of the butte. It now stretched away from the base, where he was sitting, in a dark puddle that was two or three times longer than the formation itself was high. When he tilted his head and looked up the butte's slanting wall he saw that the sky was no longer pure blue, but had taken on a tinge of gold. Sun whinnied, and Ki stood up, stepped over to the big palomino, and rubbed its velvety nose. The gesture seemed to reassure the horse, for it stamped a forefoot and tossed its head, then stood quietly again.

Moving as casually as though he were walking from the main house of the Circle Star to the bunkhouse, Ki started around the base of the towering butte toward the slit that led into the box canyon. He did not slow his leisurely pace until the edge of the opening was almost within arm's reach. Then he stopped long enough to take a quick look at the desert around the formation before dropping prone and wriggling snakelike toward his goal.

135

A strong odor of tobacco smoke drifting from the gaping slit that cut the butte from the ground to its top warned Ki that his first challenge lay directly ahead. He stopped to listen and heard only the almost inaudible brushings of cloth on cloth that told him a man was moving around just inside the opening.

His head so close to the ground that his chin occasionally brushed the dry, crusted soil, Ki advanced until he reached a spot where he could peer into the opening and see the sentry's feet. When he looked, he saw not only the man's feet, but the butt of his rifle. The feet were just beyond easy reach from the opening, but the butt of the rifle that Ki spied leaning against the wall behind them was far enough away to be out of easy reach by the sentry.

Ki saw no reason to delay his attack. Inching forward, still at ground level, he glanced at the sentry. The man was leaning against the passage wall, his head tilted up, watching the cloud of smoke he'd just puffed out whirling and dissipating in the air. Gathering his feet under him, Ki thrust himself erect, his hands already as rigid as though they had been cast from solid steel, his targets already chosen.

Before the sentry had time to react to Ki appearing in front of him as though he'd been shot up from the earth, Ki swung his right hand in a *shuto-uchi* blow that landed on the left side of the outlaw's neck just below his jawline. An instant later the edge of his left hand struck the man's right ear with a sweeping swipe that sent his head down almost to his shoulder. The popping of the outlaw's neck as the opposing blows went home could not have been heard farther than a yard away.

Ki's strikes had been delivered so quickly that the bandit had no time to cry out. His mouth was just beginning to open with a warning shout when the snapping of his spinal cord stilled him forever. He swayed for a moment, his jaw slackening and his chin dropping as his eyes glazed, then crumpled quietly to the ground.

Now that he'd gone on the offensive, Ki wasted no time. He dragged the limp body outside the opening and hurried back to complete his task. Picking up the rifle as he passed, he moved toward the end of the short passage, then as he came within a step of its exit into the canyon he dropped flat. Wriggling ahead, he stopped at the end of the slit and began studying the canyon's interior with quick side-to-side glances that almost instantly gave him an understanding of its layout.

Three of the five men left in Chaco's gang were hunkered down beside the smoldering fire, rekindling it. A fourth was on his knees beside the trickling stream, filling a pail. The fifth lounged idly a few yards from the fire, watching the others work, and Ki tagged him as the leader. All the men wore pistol belts, but Ki could see their rifles leaning against the canyon wall near the spot where a rope corral kept the horses confined.

As he swept his eyes around the towering interior wall, Ki also noticed that the area covered by the sun's rays had been reduced to a thin bright line of golden light at the very rim of the canyon's interior wall. As he brought his eyes down to the floor, he saw the shanties, and since Jessie and Ted were nowhere visible it was easy to conclude that they were confined in one of them, perhaps each one in a separate shanty.

Quickly deciding that it was unimportant whether they were together or apart, Ki dropped flat. Dragging with him the rifle he'd taken from the sentry, he started crawling *ninja*-fashion, hugging the shadow at the bottom of the canyon wall. In his loose black blouse and trousers, he might well have been just a deeper patch of the gloomy darkness that was beginning to creep from the side opposite him to the wall where the shanties stood. Nearing the first shanty, he heard a murmur of voices.

He was not close enough to the little jerry-built structure to separate the voices or distinguish any words that might have given him a clue to the identity of the speakers. Moving more slowly, he crept on until the voices were no longer merged in a single murmur. When he could distinguish between them, and recognized Jessie's familiar tones, Ki knew that he'd won the first round from the outlaws. He moved stealthily forward until he was lying at the base of the shanty, then confirmed what he was already certain was a fact.

"Jessie," he breathed. "Are you all right?"

At once Jessie's whisper reached him. "Ki?"

"Of course. Is Ted with you?"

"Yes. We've been wondering when you'd get here."

"I had to wait until it got dark enough to hide my movements. Are you tied up?"

"No. Do you want us to come out?"

"Not now. It'll be safer if I come in there."

"I'm sure there's no lock on the door. I didn't hear any click when they put us in here."

Ki wriggled around until he could see the door before replying. "No lock. Just a hasp held with a stick."

A few seconds more and Ki was inside the shanty. He stood up and Jessie threw her arms around him, pulled him to her, and kissed his cheek. Ted stepped up, groped for Ki's hand, and pressed it hard. Jessie drew back and looked at him. Even in the gloom Ki could see her smile.

"I knew you'd be here as soon as you could. Are Tim and Nora with you?"

"No. They stayed with the balloon."

"Now that you've gotten here, I suppose you have a

plan all worked out to get us away?"

"Not yet. But it won't take long to figure one out."

"Jessie kept telling me that you'd be here as soon as you could," Ted broke in. "She was certainly—" He broke off as a shot sounded from the canyon floor. It was followed by another, then the sound of pounding footsteps reached them.

"They've found the sentry," Ki told them. "I had to kill him to get into the canyon."

"Then we won't have time to make a plan," Jessie said, frowning.

"Damn!" Ted exclaimed. "We'll be sitting ducks inside this shanty! They've got guns and we haven't!"

"We have one," Ki told him. "I took the rifle that the sentry had. Wait. I'll get it before they start this way."

Dashing outside the shanty, Ki picked up the rifle from where he'd dropped it when he opened the shanty door. Even before he was back inside, a shout drew his attention to the canyon opening again. The outlaws were running away from it, toward the shanties. Chaco was in the lead and Ki saw the outlaw's hand darting for his hip.

Ki dived into the shanty as the outlaw leader's bullet tore through the wall of the flimsy structure. Gesturing for Jessie and Ted to drop to the ground, Ki hit the dirt himself. A split second later, a ragged volley of shots sounded and more bullets tore through the shanty walls.

Chapter 13

"Stay down!" Jessie warned.

Still lying facedown on the dirt floor, Jessie was pushing herself toward the open door with her feet, the rifle in her hands. She stopped short of the door and rolled to one side of it to get a better view of the canyon floor. Shouldering the rifle, she waited.

When the outlaws came within sight, she let the first one pass without shooting, but when the next man was in her sights she triggered off a shot that dropped him. The outlaw's wound wasn't fatal, for he scrabbled on the ground for a second or two and then rolled away. The shot destroyed the eagerness of his fellows, however. They scattered and scurried to get out of the line of fire from the shanty's open door. Jessie made no effort to get off a second shot. She ejected the spent shell case, but did not lever the action closed.

"Why didn't you try for another one, Jessie?" Ted asked. "It looked to me like the others were almost as close as the one you winged."

"They were," she replied. "But I don't know how many rounds there are in this gun, and the sights are strange to me. I'll do better next time, now that I know it shoots low and to the left."

"Well, at least you stopped their rush," Ted said.

"That's all I hoped to do," Jessie told him. "Because we may need every shell that's in the magazine to stop them when they rush us again."

During the exchange between Jessie and Ted, Ki had snaked up to the open door. He said over his shoulder, "Now that they know we've got a gun, they might hold off long enough to give us a chance to make some kind of plan. They've retreated to the other side of the canyon and are talking things over."

"We'd better do some talking, too," she replied, looking up for a moment while she levered bullets out of the magazine. She held out the hand in which she'd been catching the ejected shells. "You can see that whoever this rifle belonged to wasn't very smart. The magazine takes five rounds, but it only had four shells in it. These three are what we've got left."

"I have plenty of *shuriken*, Jessie," Ki volunteered. "And this place will be dark in another half our or so."

"Neither your *shuriken* or the gun will be of much use after dark," she pointed out. "And if they decide to rush this shanty, we'll be in real trouble."

"They won't be able to see any better than we can in the dark," Ted protested. "Doesn't that even things up?"

"Not as long as they've got plenty of ammunition to waste and we have to count every shot," Ki answered.

"Then we'd better think about moving as soon as we can," Jessie said matter-of-factly, as though she were talking about crossing a city street to mail a letter. She went on, "Ki, your *ninjutsu* skills should make it fairly easy for you to take a look at that next shanty. It might be a little more solidly built than this one, even if all three of them do look the same."

Ki had remained at the door, watching the outlaws, and

he said, "They're not paying any attention to us right now. Give me a minute or two, and I'll find out."

He snaked out the door and crawled along the base of the canyon wall to the shanty that stood a dozen yards away. Its construction duplicated that of the one in which they were holed up. Small saplings held together by interlaced thongs formed the walls, and Ki had a bit of trouble opening the door because the leather hinges on which it swung were cracked and sagging. The interior was bare except for a tarpaulin-draped bundle in the middle of the floor.

Lifting a corner of the canvas, Ki saw a wooden box, and even in the gloom he could read the warning sign stenciled on its side in big red letters: HANDLE WITH CARE —EXPLOSIVES.

Pulling the canvas off the box, Ki peered inside. It held a dozen sticks of dynamite bedded in sawdust, and on top of the slim red cylinders lay a coil of fuse cord and a small cloth sack. Ki did not need to open the sack, for through the cloth he could see the outlines of the stubby thimble-shaped fuses it contained.

Replacing the tarpaulin, Ki crawled back to the door and peered at the outlaws. They were still huddled around the fire. Chaco was standing with his back to Ki, his arms waving as the band listened. Though the distance was too great for Ki to hear what Chaco was saying, he could read a great deal from the bandit leader's gestures.

Chaco was pointing at different areas of the canyon, then to one or another of his followers, sketching lines in midair to indicate the course he wanted them to follow in a fresh attack on the shanty. As soon as Ki saw that the outlaws were concentrating on their instructions to the exclusion of everything else, he crawled quickly back to the shanty where Jessie and Ted were waiting.

"I think we've just won our fight," he told them. "There's a box of dynamite in that shanty, and enough fuse cord and caps to make as many bombs as we need."

"Dynamite?" Ted frowned. "I've never used it. I've heard it's awfully powerful, but real hard to handle."

"Don't worry," Jessie said. "Ki and I have used it before. We know what to do with it." She turned to Ki and went on, "We were undecided about moving to that other shanty. I think this makes up our minds for us."

"Yes." Ki nodded. "And the quicker, the better. Those outlaws have gotten over their surprise by now. They're not going to wait much longer."

Ki glanced upward, and Jessie and Ted tilted their heads to look as well. The patch of sky that was visible above the shanty's roofless walls was still bright, though there was no longer any sunshine falling on the canyon's rim.

"We've got another hour of daylight at best," Jessie said.

"If that much," Ted agreed. "And it'll get dark in here faster than outside, once the sun drops a little bit more."

"Chaco's going to try to get us out of here before it gets any darker," Ki went on. "And it won't just be a mass rush this time. From the way he's pointing out positions to his men, they'll be coming at us from different directions."

"Isn't there anyone watching us, then?" Jessie asked.

Ki shook his head. "Chaco knows he's got us bottled up. But they'll be getting into place before too long."

"One at a time, then," Jessie said. She moved to the door and looked at the outlaws for a moment. They still showed no signs of moving. Turning away from the door, she said, "Ted, you go first. Don't worry about crawling, the way Ki did. Just walk fast."

Ted nodded, and left. Jessie and Ki stood in the doorway, dividing their attention between him and the bandits.

143

They were still listening to Chaco.

"Go ahead," Ki told Jessie. "If they start toward us, I can crawl."

Jessie covered the distance to the other shanty in quick, short strides, and Ki followed her. He'd just reached the other shanty's door when the outlaws started dispersing. Stepping inside the door and peering from its shelter, Ki watched them until he saw the pattern of attack that Chaco had worked out. Two of the four able-bodied men left in the gang started walking along the wall off the canyon, then Chaco himself left the smoldering fire, followed soon afterward by the remaining pair. The man Jessie had wounded stayed at the fire and busied himself reloading his rifle.

Looking back at the pair who had been the first to move, Ki saw they'd stationed themselves well apart along the canyon wall beyond the last shanty. Chaco stopped at a spot that placed him directly across the canyon floor from the shanties, and the last two men took their places between the outlaw chief and the entrance to the canyon.

"They've spread out, Jessie," Ki said as he turned to her and Ted. "It's easy to see what Chaco's plan is. They'll more than likely start shooting as soon as he tells them to move, but they're so far apart that we'll have to waste time picking targets."

"We'd better get busy with the dynamite, then," Jessie said crisply. "Ki, if you'll start cutting the sticks into quarters, and chop off some short pieces of fuse, Ted and I will finish the bombs."

"Wait a minute!" Ted protested. "If Ki starts jabbing his knife into those sticks of dynamite, won't they blow up?"

"No," Jessie replied. "The army colonel who told me how to use dynamite said that unless it's old and unstable, the only way it can be detonated is with a fuse and a cap.

I'm worried more about us not having enough matches to light the fuses. I've got three or four in my pocket, but unless you or Ki—"

"Don't worry," Ted broke in. "I always carry a pocketful of matches, because sometimes when I go up and the air's cold I have to touch a match to the calcium chloride to start it."

"Let's get busy, then," Jessie said. "We don't have a bit of time to waste."

During the brief exchange between Jessie and Ted, Ki had already chopped a dozen short pieces of fuse and was starting to cut into one of the dynamite sticks with his razor-sharp *tanto* blade. The short, curved knife sliced the stick as though it were nothing more than soft, warm butter. Within seconds Ki handed the four short pieces to Jessie. While Ted watched, Jessie slid a cap onto the end of one of the short fuses and, with a twisting push, inserted the capped fuse into the gelatinous end of one of the stubby sections of a dynamite cylinder.

"I don't know how long these fuses will burn," she said as she guided Ted's hands while he fumbled in trying to duplicate her improvised bomb. "But my guess is they'll last less than a minute. So after you've lighted one, get rid of it fast!"

"Don't worry!" Ted assured her. "I sure don't intend to hold it any longer than I have to!"

A shout sounded from the canyon floor. Ki glanced at the dozen stubby pieces of dynamite that he'd already cut and decided they had enough for the moment. He stepped to the door and looked across the canyon floor. Chaco's command had started his men moving. They were advancing somewhat hesitantly, carrying their rifles slantwise across their chests.

Jessie struck a match and lighted the fuse of the makeshift bomb she'd just produced. The fuse spurted flame and smoke, and she tossed it toward the advancing bandits in a high arc. They were shouldering their rifles now, and Chaco was raising his voice in another harsh command as the dynamite struck the canyon floor.

"Get down on the floor!" Jessie said quickly.

Ki and Ted dropped flat and Jessie also dived to the floor just as the first shots crackled from the rifles of the advancing outlaws. Hot lead tore into the shanty's flimsy walls in the instant before Jessie's bomb went off. Then its flat booming explosion echoed and reechoed from the canyon's towering stone walls. The rifle fire ended abruptly as a cloud of yellowish smoke billowed out from the spot where the dynamite had exploded and with lightninglike speed rolled along the canyon floor to shroud the advancing outlaws.

Swirling like a thick, roiling fog, the spreading smoke filled the air. Seeing that the cloud was going to engulf the shanty in a few more moments, Ki handed Jessie another of the improvised bombs. She took it and struck another match. As a thin stream of tiny red sparks shot from the end of the fuse she tossed the bomb, aiming it toward the spot where Chaco stood, just beginning to be engulfed by the spreading smoke of the first explosion.

There was no gunfire now, but as the second piece of dynamite dropped through the spreading smoke they heard Chaco's voice raised in another harsh command. The second improvised bomb went off and the outlaw leader's words were lost in the blast and its echoes. The smoke was thicker now, and stray wisps from its edges had begun to drift into the shanty.

"Shall I throw mine now, or wait?" Ted asked.

"Throw it!" Jessie said. "Ki, get rid of yours, too! If we

146

can get this place full of smoke, we'll be able to get away before it clears!"

Ki and Ted lighted the fuses of the pieces of dynamite they were holding and tossed them into the already dense cloud of smoke that was filling the box canyon. The shouts of the outlaws were drowned when both the bombs exploded at almost the same instant, and the yellow cloud became even thicker.

"Let's go!" Jessie said quickly. "The smoke's thick enough to hide us now, but in a minute to two it'll be too thick for us to see where we're going!"

"Stay close to the back wall," Ki suggested. "It'll take us a few minutes longer to get out, but if we hurry we can pick up a couple of the outlaws' horses."

"Of course!" Jessie exclaimed. "We'll need them!"

"Only two," Ki went on. "Sun's tethered outside."

Jessie started to speak, but could only smile and swallow. Then she overcame her surge of joy and turned to Ted.

"Pick up a few sticks of that dynamite," she said. "Get the fuses and caps, too. We don't have much else to fight with. Ki, you lead the way, and I'll stay at the back to cover us with the rifle!"

By the time the three started from the shanty, the acrid yellow cloud that filled the canyon's interior was dense enough to have concealed a small army. The angry yells of the outlaws came through the smoke, but none of them could be seen.

Keeping close to the sheer stone wall, Ki led them at a half-trot through the throat-rasping yellow fumes. They splashed across the little trickling stream and, after they'd gone a bit farther, the panicked neighing of the horses led them to the rope corral. In their inbred fear of fire and smoke, the excited animals were snorting shrilly and rearing, but Jessie and Ki had soothed many panicky horses. Only a few moments after they'd grabbed the halters of two of them and made soothing noises while rubbing their muzzles, the animals had grown calm enough to lead.

Ki severed the rope forming the corral with his knife and they led the horses toward the gap that would get them to freedom. After they'd recrossed the brooklet, they could see the opening, a long, vertical rectangle of graying brightness. The smoke between them and their gate to freedom was thinning rapidly now, pushed by the wind currents that constantly flowed into the canyon through its entryway.

They were only fifty yards from their objective when, just beyond the opening, one of the outlaws came floundering out of the smoky vapor. The man was flailing his arms, trying to clear away the fumes that clouded the interior, and a moment passed before Ki recognized him as Chaco.

Jessie identified him at the same time and started to raise the rifle that she was still carrying. Ki was quicker to move than she was. He slid a *shuriken* out of his vest pocket and before Jessie could level the rifle the shining star-pointed blade was spinning through the air. Jessie caught sight of the whirling *shuriken* and held the rifle poised, ready to bring to her shoulder, but though Ki's aim had been quick it had also been unerring.

Whirling like a streak of silver, the *shuriken* took Chaco in the throat. The outlaw chief dropped the rifle he was holding and clawed frantically at the razor-edged blade. He succeeded in dislodging it, and a gush of bright arterial blood spurted as the *shuriken* dropped away.

Chaco raised his fingers to look at them, and only then saw Ki and Jessie and Ted. He tried to draw his revolver, but too much of his lifeblood had ebbed away. His knees

148

buckled and his body sagged. Then he lurched forward, fell, and lay still.

"Now we'll have to move even faster!" Jessie exclaimed. "Chaco's men will be after us as soon as the smoke in the canyon clears and they find his body!"

Looking at the opening ahead of them, Ted said, "If there was just some way to close that—" He stopped short and held up the dynamite sticks. "Here's the way! If we set these off in the gap, the outlaws left inside there won't be able to follow us! Can we do it in time?"

"We can try," Jessie replied. "You and Ki go ahead with the horses. Chaco's got something that belongs to me, and I don't want to lose it!"

She started running toward the outlaw's body. Ki watched her for a moment, then jerked his head toward the opening. "If we don't get out of here, we'll have more trouble to handle. Come on. Jessie knows what she's doing."

Ki and Ted had barely gotten clear of the short passageway when Jessie joined them. She was carrying the Colt revolver that Chaco had taken from her when she'd been captured. "Alex gave me this, if you remember, Ki. And taught me how to use it, too. I'd never have stopped regretting it if I hadn't taken the time to get it back."

Ki nodded his understanding, then said, "If Chaco broke out of the smoke, there'll be others right behind him. Use your Colt, Jessie. Stand just inside the gap there, while Ted and I set these charges."

Jessie moved quickly into the entryway while Ki and Ted, their fingers flying, capped short lengths of fuse cord and shoved them into the sticks of dynamite. Shouts, faint in the distance, were sounding inside the box canyon before they had the fuses set and the dynamite sticks piled up just inside the passage leading into the canyon.

149

"Come on out, Jessie!" Ki called. "We're ready to go!"

Jessie emerged from the gap as Ki and Ted were lighting the first fuses. As soon as the last fuse was spitting its stream of reddish sparks they moved quickly, hurrying along the curving canyon wall. Though they were waiting for the dynamite to explode, the blast seemed a long time coming, and when its booming roar finally shattered the hush and shook the ground under their feet it still caught them by surprise.

Turning to look, they saw a cloud of dust dotted with dark chunks of loose stones rising from the ground. The earth was trembling under their feet, the outside wall of the tall butte shivering from the blast's force. The intense silence in the instant that followed the blast was as impressive as the explosion itself, then the pattering of stones and debris falling and thudding into the ground broke the spell.

"I'd sure hate to be up in a balloon above something like that," Ted said, shaking his head as he watched the dust cloud slowly fading away. With a look of surprise on his face, he turned to Ki and went on, "You know, that balloon is the only thing in the world I own, and I haven't even asked you about it, Ki. Is it all right?"

"Perfectly safe," Ki told him. "It was flat when we got to it, but Tim and Nora are taking care of it. It'll be in the wagon and ready to go when we join them."

"And then," Jessie said, "We'll get back to Silver City and finish the job we started without wasting any more time!"

Chapter 14

"I never really thought I'd be this glad to see Silver City, Ki," Jessie remarked as Ki reined in his horse beside Sun at the top of the long, steep grade and joined her in looking down at the town. "But I'll be just as glad to leave it and go back to the Circle Star as soon as we can clear up that problem at the mine."

"What bothers me is that if our suspicions about Dan Coats are right, he may have taken advantage of the time we were away to cover his tracks," Ki said.

"That's occurred to me, too." She nodded. "But remember, the assay office in Santa Rita keeps records of the amount of ore they process at the smelter there."

"It'll take me about a day to go through the mine's books," Ki told Jessie. "Then we can ride over to Santa Rita and see if their reports show a different story."

"We need that day to rest up a bit after all the traveling we've had to do," Jessie said. "And it'll take at least two or three days for Ted and Tim and Nora to get the balloon back in shape."

"You're really going up again?"

"Why, certainly!"

"I thought that wild ride you and Ted had might have changed your mind about balloons being used the way he claims they can."

"Remember how horse wranglers treat tenderfeet who're just learning to ride, Ki." Jessie smiled. "When one of them gets bucked off, the wrangler makes him get right back in the saddle and try again."

Ki nodded. "That's just what my teachers did. When I had trouble learning the moves they made me repeat them time after time until I could use them almost automatically."

"Besides," Jessie went on, "It's not every day that a balloon gets caught in a levanter. There's a good chance that what happened to us will never happen again."

Plodding hoofbeats and the creaking of wheels and harness interrupted their conversation as the wagon drew close to the top of the grade. Tim reined in.

"I guess the old saying's right," he sighed. "The last hill's always the steepest."

"At least we'll be sleeping in a bed tonight," Nora said. "The ground seems to've gotten a little bit harder every night since we started back, and sleeping on the floor of that boxcar last night was even worse."

"Our wild ride certainly proved one thing, Jessie," Ted observed. "A balloon can certainly cover a lot of miles in a shorter time than either a horse or a train. When do you want to go up and finish the job we were starting?"

"As soon as the balloon's ready," Jessie told him.

"We can go up tomorrow, if you like," Ted said. "Tim and Nora put the bag in perfect shape while they were waiting for us to get back."

"Ki and I are going to be busy for two or three days," Jessie said. "But I'm sure you can put that time to good use, even if it's just relaxing and getting ready. We'll settle on a schedule tomorrow, but let's get on into Silver City now and enjoy a good supper and real beds."

• • •

"I guess it's just as well that I put off going up in the balloon with Ted for a day or two," Jessie told Ki as they wound through a stand of straggly pines on their way to Santa Rita. "You worked much faster than I'd thought you would in getting the figures together."

"Coats seems to have kept the production records in good order," Ki said thoughtfully. "But I remember something Alex told me a long time ago. He said that he was always a bit suspicious of a bookkeeper whose ledgers didn't have a minor mistake or two."

"And Coats's books look too perfect?"

Ki nodded. "Not a single entry in them has been changed or scratched through."

"I don't want to do Dan an injustice, but—" Jessie broke off and pointed to the strip of sky that was visible above the trail. A bank of dark gray clouds was rolling toward them, covering the clear blue sky. "Those look like rain clouds to me."

"They do, at that," Ki agreed. "But I suppose it must rain now and then, even in this dry country."

"Did you bring a slicker, Ki? I didn't."

"Neither did I. But a rain in this country never lasts very long, and neither of us is going to melt if we get wet."

"I don't think we have much farther to go. We ought to be in Santa Rita in another hour at most." Jessie looked up at the sky again. "But the clouds are coming toward us awfully fast."

Even as Jessie spoke a light patter of raindrops began to spatter on the ground. The shower sprinkled them lightly and moved on, but before they'd gone another quarter-mile they saw a sheet of rain shimmering between earth and sky, racing in their direction. The strip of blue sky between them and the clouds disappeared rapidly and then the rain hit with a sudden angry sweep of chilly wind.

153

Lowering their heads, the horses plodded on while the rain grew more and more intense and the wind increased. The sparse branches of the pines lining the trail were whipping now, and what had been drops of rain turned into sheets of shimmering white that dashed stingingly against their faces.

Raising her voice to be heard over the whistling of wind in the pine branches, Jessie said, "We'll really be soaked if this keeps up very long!"

"We wouldn't be any better off if we stopped, or turned off the trail to get under the trees," Ki replied. He looked from one side of the trail to the other. "If we—"

He stopped suddenly as Jessie broke in to say, "Look, Ki! I think I see some kind of building or house right over there!"

Ki bent forward, blinking to free his eyes of the filming effects of the rain. He said, "It looks deserted, but it might give us a little shelter until this blow passes."

Jessie was already reining Sun off the trail. Ki followed her. As they drew closer, they saw the wall of an adobe house, one that had obviously been long abandoned. Its windows were without panes or shutters, its doorway yawned blackly, and the door hung inside by its bottom hinge.

"It's deserted, and might not have a roof, but it'll keep the wind from hitting us," Ki called, raising his voice to be heard above the whistling of the chilling wind through the trees.

"It can't be worse than it is out here," she replied as she swung off Sun's back and started for the door opening.

Ki followed her quickly. Inside, they found that the roof of the long, narrow room they'd entered was broken in a few spots, but generally intact. In one corner a domed adobe fireplace yawned, and a few lengths of broken pine

154

limbs, stripped of their twigs, lay beside it. A heap of black coals stood in the center of the fireplace. Though the wind whistled through the door and the glassless windows and brought gusts of rain with it, the corner where the fireplace stood was dry.

"It looks like we're not the first to take shelter here," Jessie said. She pointed to the blackened coals in the fireplace and the branches that lay on the floor in front of it. "Even though this rain might not last long, a fire would sure feel good right now."

"All it takes is a match." Ki smiled. "And I've got plenty of them in my match safe."

He picked up a piece of one of the broken branches and began raking the black, dead coals in the bottom of the fireplace to its sides. When he'd cleared the hearth, he started breaking up the smaller branches, then took his *tanto* knife from its sheath and sliced slivers off the branches for kindling.

While Ki whittled, Jessie began walking around the room, moving from one of the windows to the next, glancing at the rain, which was still pelting down. Ki began heaping the little pile of shavings he'd created into a tepee shape in the center of the hearth, and as he worked the yawning chimney opening in the center caught his eye.

Leaning forward, he twisted his head to look up and make sure the flue was unobstructed. At the point where the domed top straightened into the chimney, he saw a sheet of scorched paper that had lodged against a protruding adobe brick, and poked it with the end of the branch he'd been shaving. The paper floated down and settled on the hearth.

Ki was pushing the parched brown paper with the stick to add it to the kindling he'd shaved off when he noticed that, while the edges of the paper were charred, its center portion was still intact. It was filled with columns of figures, and heat had turned the ink a deep brown. Idly, he bent down to look at the columns. Even at his first glance they seemed familiar to him, and he studied them more closely.

"Jessie," he said after a moment. "Come look at this. I think I may have found something very interesting."

Her eyebrows lifting in surprise, Jessie stepped up to the hearth, asking, "What on earth is it, Ki?"

"I'm not really sure. I just wondered if you'd get the same feeling I have, that we've seen sheets like this before. Tell me whether or not I'm just imagining something."

After she'd examined the paper for a moment, Jessie told him, "I don't think you're imagining anything, Ki. But how did that paper get here? Where did you find it? And why—"

"One thing at a time," Ki broke in. "I looked up the chimney to be sure it was clear and saw this lodged on a brick in the flue. I poked it and it fell down. I was about to push it in with the kindling when it started looking familiar."

"It does look like something I've seen before," she agreed slowly. Then she looked from the paper to Ki, her eyes wide, and went on, "The ledger sheets you were working on with Dan Coats, Ki! It looks just like them."

"It did to me, too, but I didn't want to say anything that might influence you to agree with me." Ki stood up. "That copy of the mine ledger pages I made is in my saddlebag. Wait just a minute while I get it."

Ki dashed outside and came back after a moment carrying his dripping saddlebags and shaking drops of water off his chin. He opened one of the bags, took out a sheaf of folded papers, and unfolded them on the floor in front of the fireplace. He and Jessie dropped to their knees and bent over them, Jessie holding the scorched sheet from the fire-place next to the sheets Ki had brought in.

"They look alike," Jessie said slowly. "Allowing for the charred edges."

"Of course, all the ledger sheets I've seen are just about the same." Ki frowned. "We can't tell from this one I found whether it has the same color of ink, either in its printed lines or the figures somebody's written."

"This certainly looks like Dan's writing to me," Jessie said.

"It does to me, too," Ki said, nodding.

"But what's this sheet doing here?"

"I've been asking myself that question ever since I saw it, Jessie. And I can only think of one answer."

"I'm sure yours is the same I've got in mind. Especially because of the suspicions that brought us here."

"That sheet was lodged very loosely in the flue," Ki said. "It can't have been there very long. And the only person who could have left it here is Coats."

"But when, Ki? And why?"

"When is an answer we might never know. But you know the why as well as I do, Jessie, at least part of it."

"Yes," she replied. "Coats intended to burn it. And the only reason he had for burning it was because the figures on it don't jibe with the ones in the ledger he's showed us."

"If you want to guess a little more, Coats probably knows about this house. He goes to Santa Rita pretty regularly. My own guess is that he's stopped here to burn more than one sheet like this, and this one we found is fairly recent."

"Then the burned sheet shows the real production fig-ures, Ki. And these figures wouldn't agree with those in the ledger at the mine, the ones you copied on this new sheet. But the figures that Coats shows in the reports he

157

sends to the Circle Star are the same as the ones he's shown us in the mine office."

Ki was silent for a moment, then he said, "Do you agree with my guess that Coats has been stopping here regularly on his way back from the smelter? You've mentioned that his reports have shown production dropping for quite some time."

Jessie nodded. "This is the answer we came here to find, Ki. Of course, we won't know the whole answer until we've gone on to the smelter and checked their figures against his."

"We'll know that soon enough," Ki said. "As soon as the rain stops we'll get on to Santa Rita. And I'm as sure as it's possible to be that we'll find the proof we're looking for in the smelter's records.

"I don't think we'll get to Santa Rita tonight, though," Ki went on, looking out of the glassless window at the steady downpour. "I'll go out and unsaddle the horses and get them into the best place I can find for them. This cabin's not much, but it's the only shelter we're likely to find, so we might as well plan on staying here tonight."

"When the mine here was producing, Santa Rita must have been quite some town," Jessie observed as she and Ki started down the main street.

They were riding between rows of adobe buildings in various stages of decay. Some had crumbled to shapeless heaps of disintegrated bricks, others had only parts of their walls standing. A few showed signs of fairly recent habitation; their walls were intact but the doors, windows, and frames had been removed, giving these openings the appearance of lidless eyes staring blankly at the rutted street.

Some of the few that were still inhabited were suffering from peeling paint on doors and windows, but a few were still neat and well-kept, with curtains at the windows and doors, and window frames painted bright blue. The street ahead was deserted except for two or three ragged children who had huddled together in front of one of the houses and were gazing at the newcomers with undisguised curiosity.

"It looks a lot better from a distance than it does when you get closer to it," Ki agreed. "But it's been twenty or thirty years since the lode of the big mine petered out, so I suppose this kind of decay was to be expected."

"I can imagine Silver City looking like this someday, if our mine and all the other new ones were closed down," Jessie said thoughtfully. They reined their horses to a halt in front of a big cut-stone building beyond the center of the deteriorating town. "This fits the description we got of the assay office, and even it looks a little seedy."

"It's certainly not very new." Ki smiled, indicating the white cornerstone engraved with the royal arms of Spain and the date A.D. 1752. "But I understand that the silver mines are a couple of hundred years older. They were being worked by the Indians before the Spaniards got here."

"That's older than I like to think about," Jessie said as they went into the building.

A counter ran the width of the large, open interior. Behind it an aging man was bending over a small, round iron stove. He looked up, saw Jessie and Ki, and came to the counter.

"Can I help you folks?" he asked.

"We're looking for Mr. Edgar Green," Jessie replied. "He is the manager, isn't he?"

"Well, ma'am, he was till just over a year ago," the man replied. "But then he took sick and died. Mr. Jim Talley's the manager now."

"We'll talk to him, then," Jessie said. "My name is Jessica Starbuck. I own the Starbuck mine in Silver City, and I need to get confirmation of some assay reports."

"Well, I'm real sorry, but Mr. Talley's not here, Miss Starbuck," the clerk replied. "He had to make a trip down to El Paso. I don't look for him back until tomorrow or the next day."

"Talley," Ki said thoughtfully. "Is he related to the new town marshal in Silver City?"

"You mean young Will?" the clerk asked, then without waiting for a reply added, "He's Jim's brother." He turned back to Jessie. "If it's just figures you want, Miss Starbuck, I guess I can oblige you."

"That will be a big help," Jessie said. "What I want to see is the original figures of assays made of the ore from my mine during the past year.''

"Well, that ain't a lot to dig out," the clerk said. "Mr. Talley keeps the figures for all the mines on separate sheets. I'll just get out your file, and you can sit down at that table over yonder and go through them."

Stepping over to a filing case that stood at the end of the counter, the clerk opened a drawer and selected one of the files that filled it. He handed the file to Jessie.

"You'll find what you need right there," he said.

"Thank you." Jessie nodded.

She took the file and, followed by Ki, went to the table the clerk had indicated. Ki put the papers he'd taken from his saddlebag on the table beside the assay-office reports, and he and Jessie bent over them. The ruled sheets used by the mine were almost identical in form to those of the assay office. Each covered a month's period, and listed the weight of the raw ore delivered to the smelter each week, then in a separate entry showed the quantity of ore removed for the assay tests.

160

Another column showed the percentage of metal recovered from each ounce of raw ore, then in separate columns were the figures giving the percentage of silver recovered per ounce of ore as well as the percentages of gold and copper, the two trace metals almost universally found in silver ores. In the final columns the quantities of each of the metals recovered by smelting and delivered to the mine's owners were given.

Jessie and Ki began comparing the delivery figures on the Starbuck mine's ledgers to those in the assay reports. After they'd checked the results for the first few shipments, Jessie looked up from the ledger pages, a frown on her face.

"These figures are just the same as those in the ledgers you got at the mine office, Ki," she said. "Maybe the mine production is just dwindling. We might be coming to the end of the silver lode."

"It's possible," Ki agreed. "But there's something that bothers me about these figures. The quantity of silver being recovered keeps going down, but the amounts of gold and copper stay the same. Doesn't it stand to reason that they'd fall off just like the silver recovery does?"

"Of course they should," she said. "Except for the fact that the trace metals are reversed, the ratios should be just like the ones from the copper mines Alex developed in Montana, where the trace ores are silver and gold. Those ratios don't change, and I don't understand why they've changed here in New Mexico."

Ki picked up the scorched ledger page that he'd found in the cabin chimney. He looked at it for a moment, frowning, then laid it beside the pages from the assay office and the Silver City mine.

"Let's see how these compare," he suggested.

A few moments later, after they'd compared the percentages on the fire-scorched ledger sheet, Jessie and Ki again exchanged glances.

"This sheet you found in the cabin shows a great deal more silver being recovered than the other two," Jessie said, her voice thoughtful. "But the ratios of silver and copper are the same. My hunch was right, Ki. And I'll bet that if we had the real figures we'd find that Dan Coats has been stealing silver from the mine for the past year."

"This sheet I found shows something else, too." Ki picked up the burned ledger page and held it close to one of those the clerk had taken from his file. "These sheets are in the same handwriting, so Jim Talley must have filled in both of them. That means he's falsifying the assay-office records so they'll agree with the sheets Coats keeps at the mine."

"I don't think Coats could have worked this scheme out by himself, Ki." Jessie frowned. "And he certainly couldn't have carried it out unless Jim Talley was in it with him. You know, I'm beginning to think it might have been Talley's idea."

"Jim Talley," Ki said. "The brother of Will Talley. Don't you suppose that's why Will got himself appointed marshal of Silver City, Jessie? He's there to keep an eye on Coats."

"Oh, certainly," Jessie agreed. "Let's ask the clerk a question or two, Ki. I'd like to know a lot more about Mr. Jim Talley!"

Chapter 15

Carrying the assay office's ledger, Jessie went to the counter and called to the clerk, "We're through with your file, now. And thank you very much for your help."

"Why, it wasn't any trouble, Miss Starbuck. I'm sorry Mr. Talley wasn't here, but I'm glad you found out what you was looking for."

"Your ledger sheets are certainly very neat," Jessie said as she handed the pages to the clerk. "Your handwriting is so clear that we didn't have a bit of trouble."

"I'm afraid I can't take credit for that," the man told her. "I just scribble down the figures on a scrap of paper and then Mr. Talley copies them on these ledger sheets."

"I'm sorry we didn't get to meet him," Jessie said, keeping her voice carefully casual. "Does he go to El Paso often?"

"Not real often, no, ma'am. About once a month is all. And he ought to be getting back tomorrow sometime."

"We'll just miss him by a day, then," Jessie said. "I suppose he has business with the main office of the Department of the Interior?" Then, before the clerk could reply, Jessie shook her head and went on, "But that wouldn't take him to El Paso, would it? All the federal offices for New Mexico territory are in Santa Fe."

"Oh, he goes to El Paso on private business," the clerk said. "Can't say I blame him for going, either. Santa Rita's pretty much a ghost town these days. If I was a younger man, I'd enjoy a trip to El Paso once a month myself."

"I'm sure you would." Jessie smiled. "Well, I'll look forward to meeting Mr. Talley the next time I come to Santa Rita. Ki and I are going to be at the mine for quite a while, and I'm sure we'll have a reason to come back here again."

"You spread that on pretty thick, Jessie," Ki said as they reached the street and mounted their horses.

"I intended to. I want Mr. Jim Talley to be worried about our visit here."

"Stirring up the animals." He nodded. "Not enough to panic them, but enough to tempt them to do something foolish."

"It's worked before," Jessie replied, then added, "I can stop Dan Coats from stealing silver just by firing him, but that's not good enough. I want to put the Talley brothers where they belong, too."

"Yes, of course," Ki agreed. "Crooks must be punished, to discourage other crooks. All three of them will have to be put in jail."

"You may have had the same thought that occurred to me, Ki," she went on. "Jim Talley must have a reason for making those monthly visits to El Paso."

"To deposit the silver he and his confederates have stolen, of course," Ki said. "He wouldn't risk going to Albuquerque or Santa Fe, but El Paso's close enough to be convenient, far enough away to be private, and big enough to have large banks where a sizable deposit of silver wouldn't attract attention."

"Let's do some planning, then," Jessie suggested. "I'm sure we can find a way to catch them, or to surprise them into confessing. Right now, though, I don't have any ideas."

"Neither do I, but between us, we ought to be able to come up with one."

"It's a long ride back to Silver City," Jessie said. "And by the time we get there we should be able to work out a plan that will break up their little scheme. From what the assay-office clerk said, Talley won't be back until at least tomorrow. That will give me time to go up with Ted again and finish the job we were starting when that levanter interrupted us."

"I really think we've got a workable plan at last, Ki," Jessie said as she and Ki started down the long slope that led from the Starbuck mine to Silver City.

Below them, scattered lights were beginning to show in the little town that lay at the end of the long, gentle incline. The horses were already trying to move faster as they sensed with the mysterious instinct of animals long associated with man that they were ending a long day of constant movement and that food and water and rest lay just ahead.

"Yes," Ki agreed. "As soon as we've had supper, I'll go find Will Talley and do the rest of the seed-planting."

"There's only one thing that bothers me, Ki. If Jim Talley is late in getting back from El Paso, or doesn't take the bait I left with the clerk in Santa Rita, our plan might not work."

"We don't have to worry about the timing, Jessie," Ki said reassuringly. "We'll finish baiting the trap and set it when we get back to Silver City. The silver thieves will walk into it if we're patient. All we're got to do is wait a day or two."

"I could tell that Dan Coats got very uncomfortable

165

when we mentioned our trip to Santa Rita," Jessie said, and smiled.

"So I noticed." Ki nodded. "He was too smart to ask any questions, but his looks certainly gave away what he must have been thinking."

"Let him worry overnight," Jessie said. "If our plan works out, he'll be worrying about a trial and prison sentence by this time tomorrow." ·

They rode on in companionable silence as the darkness grew deeper. By the time they reached Silver City the lights spilling across Bullard Street from the stores that lined it on both sides provided the only illumination. They reined in at the hotel and Ki held out his hand.

"Give me Sun's reins when you dismount," he said. "I'll take him and ride on to the livery stable. The town marshal's office is just a few steps from it. I'll stop in and talk to Will Talley. We want to get our plan working without wasting any time."

"Thank you, Ki," Jessie replied as she swung out of her saddle. As she turned back to Ki after lifting off her saddlebags she went on, "I think I'll go on up to my room and have my supper brought up there. A sponge bath while I'm waiting is just what I need to relax me before I go to bed."

Ki rode on to the livery stable and, after leaving the horses, walked past the stableyard to the marshal's office. Will Talley looked up from his desk, his face betraying his surprise at the unexpected visit.

"What brings you here, Ki?" he asked. "I hope there's not any trouble out at Miss Starbuck's mine."

"Not trouble of the kind that you're probably thinking of," Ki replied. "All I can tell you is that Jessie asked me to stop in and make sure you'll be around for the next few days."

"What's the matter?" Talley frowned. "Trouble at the

mine? Did something happen out there to alarm her?"

"I'm not sure," Ki told him, letting a bit of uncertainty tinge his voice. "You know, I just work for Miss Starbuck. She doesn't always confide in me about everything she's thinking. All I know is that while Jessie and I were on the way back from Santa Rita this evening—"

"You and Miss Starbuck have been to Santa Rita?" Talley broke in, frowning.

"Yes, she had some business in the assay office there. But she didn't choose to confide in me about that, either. All she told me was to find out for sure that you'd be in town if she needed to call you in."

"Call me in for what?"

"I'd like to know that myself," Ki answered blandly. "But I suppose we'll both learn when Jessie decides it's time."

"Well, you can tell Miss Starbuck that I'm not planning to go anywhere. Whenever she needs help, I'll be on hand."

"I'm sure that'll relieve her mind." Ki nodded. "Now that I've delivered Jessie's message, I'm going back to the hotel and get some supper. That road from Santa Rita's a very bad one, but I guess you know that."

For a moment Talley hesitated uncertainly. Forearmed with the knowledge he and Jessie had acquired in Santa Rita, Ki could tell that the young marshal was trying to decide whether to say anything about his brother, and recognized the moment when he'd made a decision.

"Yes," Talley said. "I've been there a few times. But my job here doesn't take me to Santa Rita very often."

"Of course," Ki replied blandly. "I'll say goodnight then, Marshal Talley, and tell Jessie she needn't worry about your being on hand if she should have to call on you."

• • •

Jessie was crossing the hotel lobby when Ted Sanders turned away from the registration desk and saw here. He hurried to meet her. "I've been worried about you, Jessie!" he exclaimed. "I didn't realize until I'd asked the desk clerk that you'd gone to Santa Rita."

"It wasn't a trip I'd planned," Jessie told him. "Ki and I left so hurriedly that I didn't have a chance to tell you."

"We certainly haven't had much time together since we left that outlaw hideout," Ted went on.

Jessie heard much more than his words. The eagerness in his voice and the yearning look in his eyes revealed the message the young balloonist was trying to send her.

"You know how busy we've been," Jessie replied. "Ki and I have been trying to solve a puzzle, and that's really what we came here to do, Ted. Experimenting with your balloon was just part of the reason for asking you to come with us."

"You spend a lot of time with Ki, Jessie. I can't keep from wondering—"

"You don't have to wonder," she broke in. "Ki is my good friend, nothing more. He was my father's friend and helper, and after Alex was murdered he stayed on to help me."

"I see," Ted said, his voice and face showing that he still didn't understand the complex relationship between Jessie and Ki. "But where does that leave me?"

"Why—" Jessie began, then stopped short when she saw the hurt and puzzled expression on his face. She asked, "Have you had supper yet, Ted?"

He shook his head. "No. I was waiting for you. I hoped we could eat together this evening."

By now Jessie had reached a decision. She nodded and told him, "I think that's a wonderful idea, Ted. Suppose you go to the dining room and order our supper. While you're doing that, I'll go upstairs and freshen up. We'll have supper in my room."

"Alone? Without Ki or Tim or Nora?"

"Of course we'll eat alone," she assured him. "Wouldn't you rather eat in my room instead of the dining room?"

"You know I would, Jessie!"

"Go on and order, then. It'll take them ten or fifteen minutes to get our food ready, and that's about how long I need to get rid of the travel dirt I've picked up."

Jessie went up the stairs and into her room. It was dim in the light that filtered through the open door, and she crossed the room to the dresser, dropped her saddlebags beside it, and picked up the match safe that stood beside the lamp. Lifting the chimney, she struck the match and touched it to the wick, then closed the door and shed her traveling jacket as she stepped back to the bureau.

Moving with swift efficiency, she slipped out of the riding boots and rough clothes that she'd worn on the trip to Santa Rita. Stepping over to the washstand that stood along one wall, she poured water from the pitcher into the washbowl.

Taking off her traveling clothes, Jessie hung them on a hook in the wardrobe. She had a sponge bath and slipped into the soft, clinging silk negligee that was one of the touches of home she allowed herself on the trips she made to such isolated places as Silver City. She was standing in front of the mirror combing the wind-tangles out of her hair when a muffled tapping sounded on the door.

Turning away from the mirror, she called, "I didn't lock the door, Ted. Come on in."

"I'm afraid I can't turn the knob," Ted called. "This tray I'm carrying is too big and clumsy."

Hurrying to the door, Jessie opened it. Ted was holding a big oval tray, his arms spread wide apart to grasp it. The tray was barely large enough to accommodate the covered casserole, silver coffeepot, and china plates, cups, and saucers that it held. He slid through the door sideways and put the tray on the square table that stood in the center of the room.

"I hope you like chicken stew," he said as he turned back to Jessie. "It sounded like the best dish they had downstairs."

"Chicken stew will be a nice change from beef," Jessie said, smiling. "But why didn't you have one of the waiters bring that tray up?"

"I—well, I wasn't sure that you'd want anybody to know we were going to eat together in your room."

"It wouldn't have embarrassed me a bit," Jessie said. "But it was sweet and thoughtful of you, just the same."

She stepped up to Ted to kiss him. Then, as he wrapped his arms around her and their lips met, what Jessie had intended to be a brief, lip-brushing thank-you kiss became something more. As Ted's arms pressed her closer and his tongue slid through their clinging lips to find hers, she felt the bulge growing at his crotch and slid one hand down to caress it through the fabric of his trousers.

They clung together until breathlessness forced them apart. Ted leaned back, looking with worship in his face at Jessie's shining eyes and moist red lips. He said, "This is the first time we've been alone since we started back from the outlaw hideout, Jessie. You're not mad at me for what happened there, are you?"

"Of course not, Ted! I enjoyed it as much as you did, but on the way back there wasn't any way for us to be together, with Nora and Tim and Ki along."

"That's what I kept reminding myself, but since we've been here you haven't had much time for me, either."

"Work's gotten in the way," Jessie said. Then she

looked at the tray on the table and went on, her voice soft, "I was hungry before you kissed me, but now—" A mischievous smile growing on her face, she went on, "You make the choice, Ted. Which would you rather have first? Me, or supper?"

Ted's surprised look became a smile. Pulling her into his arms again, he said, "You ought to know the answer to that, Jessie. Supper's a—well, something I have every day. I can't say the same thing about you. You're special."

As their lips met once again, Jessie quickly unbuckled Ted's belt and began unbuttoning his fly. Ted held their kiss until both were once more breathless, then brushed his lips down the pulsing column of her throat and along her softly rounded shoulders, pushing the silk of her negligee aside as he traced her silken skin with his quivering tongue. By the time Jessie had worked the buttons of his trousers free, Ted's lips had bared her breasts and his tongue was caressing their budded tips.

Jessie's pulse was racing now, and she lost no time in moving her fingers to Ted's shirt, unbuttoning it and freeing the buttons of his underwear at the same time. She held herself away from him while stripping his shirt and undersuit down over his hips. When his erection jutted free she trapped the rigid column of flesh between their bodies and pressed her hips against his as she leaned down to whisper to him, "Why are we wasting time standing here, when the bed's so close?"

Instead of replying, Ted lifted Jessie and, with a single long step, covered the small distance to the bed. He lowered Jessie gently, letting her weight pull him down until he was crouched above her. Wordlessly, Jessie smiled and spread her thighs. Then Ted lunged with a long swift stroke that brought a cry of delight from Jessie's lips.

For the first few moments after his deep penetration,

171

Ted drove furiously, and Jessie brought her hips up to meet his rapid thrusts. Then the memory of their first brief, frenzied encounter flashed into her mind. She wrapped her legs tightly around his hips, pressing him to her until his fierce lunges were slowed and he'd fallen into a slower, more measured tempo.

Jessie began caressing Ted's pulsing throat in the manner taught her by the old Japanese courtesan to whom Alex had entrusted her instruction in the ways of a woman with a man.

With her lips she sought the soft, pulsing spot where throat and shoulder joined, and where sensitive nerves lay shallow. Burying her face in the little throbbing hollow, she let her tongue wander over his skin until she felt the quivers that rippled through his body increase to match those which were beginning to shake her.

Using her own mounting pleasure as a gauge, Jessie kept up her caresses as long as she dared, then moved her head away and locked Ted's hips with her legs until he could no longer drive with long fierce lunges.

"What's the matter, Jessie?" Ted whispered in a puzzled tone. "Aren't you—"

"Yes," she broke in. "I am enjoying this. So much that I don't want it to end too soon. Let's lie still for just a little while, Ted."

After they'd lain motionless for a few moments and Jessie could feel the shivers that had shaken Ted dying away, she signaled with a twist of her hips for him to resume his stroking. Ted started slowly, but the delay had made him impatient, and in a moment he was lunging into her again with urgent, driving strokes. When Jessie began responding involuntarily, twisting her hips and bringing them up to meet his fierce thrusts, she knew the time was right.

Surrendering herself to her feelings, she met Ted's

172

lunges with an urgency of her own. When he gasped and shuddered in the final moments before jetting, Jessie's soft body rippled as wave after wave of sensation swept her to the heights, peaked, and ebbed as Ted lurched in a final deep penetration. Then they lay still, bodies still entwined, and only the gasping of their exhausted breathing filled the room.

Chapter 16

"I think I stirred Will Talley up enough yesterday evening to start him moving," Ki told Jessie as they sat at breakfast in the hotel dining room. "When I got back to the hotel yesterday evening you weren't in here or in the lobby, so I thought you must be resting in your room, and didn't want to disturb you."

"Your guess was a good one, Ki. I felt grimy after our trip to Santa Rita, so I went upstairs to freshen up. The idea of bed was so tempting that I never did get around to dinner. But I'd like to hear what you told Will Talley."

"It wasn't so much what I told him as what I hinted at." Ki smiled. "He'll imagine a lot more than I could have told him."

"Enough for him to send word to his brother to come here?"

"I think so. Certainly enough for him to feel like he has to talk to Coats. We'll just have to watch both of them and see what they do."

Jessie frowned. "I arranged for Ted to take me up in the balloon this morning," she said. "I thought I might as well use today for the look I want to take at the area around the mine."

"It's too soon for Talley to do much today," Ki said.

"Go ahead with whatever you've planned. I need to go out to the mine and get Coats stirred up as well as Talley."

"After you've talked to him, ride on past the mine about a half-mile. Ted thinks that's the best place to take the balloon up. I imagine that he and Ted and Nora are already out there, getting everything ready."

"Then I'll ride as far as the mine with you, have my talk with Coats, and come join you."

"Good." Jessie glanced at Ki's plate and saw it was empty. "If you're through eating, we can leave right now."

Riding in the companionable silence of friends long accustomed to being together, Jessie and Ki parted company at the mine. She rode on to the spot where the balloon was being readied, while Ki turned and swung off his horse at the mine office.

"How come Miss Starbuck ain't along with you?" Coats asked as Ki entered the office.

"She's going to have another try at prospecting from the balloon. But there are a few things she wanted me to talk over with you, if you've got time."

"I hope it ain't anything very important," Coats said.

Ki shook his head, his face blandly guileless, and replied, "Just a few sets of figures that Jessie and I ran into yesterday at the assay office in Santa Rita."

"Maybe I ought've gone there with you. Seeing as I'm on the job here all the time, I imagine I know the ropes better'n you or Miss Starbuck. I could've saved you and her some trouble."

"We didn't really have any trouble," Ki told Coats. "In fact, Jessie and I were both surprised how quickly and easily we found the figures we needed."

Coats was silent for a moment, then he said, "Ki, I just ain't very chipper today. Must've been something I had for supper that's making my belly feel all upset." There was a nervous edge to his voice that hadn't been present when he'd greeted Ki. He went on, "I just don't feel up to going over a lot of figures right now."

"Well, if you don't feel up to talking right now, we can wait until this afternoon, or even tomorrow," Ki told the mine superintendent.

"Let's do that, if you don't mind. I think I'd better go into town and see if I can't get something from the doctor that'll make me feel better."

"I'll ride on up the road, then, and watch Jessie go up in the balloon," Ki said. "They're getting it ready now."

"Whereabouts is this place she'll be going up?"

"About a mile to the north," Ki replied. "It's an open spot just off the road."

"You go ahead, then." Coats nodded. "And we'll have our talk tomorrow, for sure."

"You're not nervous, are you, Jessie?" Ted asked as the balloon gained altitude.

"A little bit, I guess," she admitted, looking down at the foreshortened figures of Nora and Tim, who still stood beside the wagon. She waved at them before going on, "But I hope we don't run into another of those crazy winds."

"There's not much chance of that," the balloonist replied. "Levanters don't occur very often."

"We only have to be high enough to see what the ground is like beyond the lode the miners are working now," Jessie reminded him. "Look for the paths the ore carts have made from the diggings to the road."

"We're not high enough yet to watch a lot of ground," Ted told her. "And this ground current's taking us the wrong way. I'd better put more hot air into the bag and take us up a bit more, at least until we get into a crosswind that'll take us in the right direction."

Ted busied himself with the calcium chloride container while Jessie continued to scan the ground. After a few minutes the balloon began rising slowly, and Jessie watched the horizon expanding on all sides. Suddenly she realized that she was enjoying the sensation of floating free above the earth.

"Will we be able to see the kind of formations we're looking for if we go up higher?" she asked Ted.

"Of course, unless we get up too high," he replied. "And I'll be careful not to do that. But we've got to rise high enough to get a good view of all these hills."

"Since the air's so quiet, are we going to be able to find a current that'll take us over the area I want to look at?"

"Well, you've been up twice now, and except for the time we were caught in the levanter you've seen how I can change direction by finding the right current," Ted reminded her. "I'm not familiar yet with the regular currents that form over these mountains, though. It might take us a little time."

"There doesn't seem to be much wind today."

"No. That little storm you and Ki ran into going to Santa Rita the other day left calm air behind it. We shouldn't see much change in the weather during the next few days."

By now they'd risen high enough to give Jessie a view of the mine. She studied it and the area around it, and discovered that the terrain looked very different when viewed from a perspective other than the familiar one at ground level. The office building now appeared to be half the size it was when she stood in front of it, and from the height the balloon had now reached the road between Silver City and Santa Rita that ran close to the office looked much less inviting that it did from the back of a horse. It wound like a giant wriggling earthworm, a brown streak cutting a narrow swath through the green branches of the trees.

Viewed from above, the growth that seemed so scanty on the ground acted as a dense shield that hid the earth's surface. Tim and Nora were no longer visible now; the balloon's slow drift as it rose had put them beneath the screening trees. The mineshafts showed as dark spaces, narrow rectangles rather than the roughly square openings that they were in reality. The shafts were strung out along one side of the snaking road on which two or three ore carts were moving slowly.

Connected by the haulage road, the low, humped hills into which the mine's tunnels were cut formed an undulating spine that bound the individual shafts into a unit. Jessie turned to Ted and pointed to the row of humps.

"Just imagine those little hills forming a single ridge," she suggested. "That's what we're looking for. A long time ago all the hills that have silver under them were probably just one long ridge. The geologists I've talked to say that all this country has been changed during the years by earthquakes."

"I'll be watching for ridges and hills, then," Ted said. "We'll be seeing a much bigger area when we go higher."

As the balloon continued ascending, a flicker of movement between the trees on the brow of a hill almost directly under the basket caught Jessie's eye. In that area the trees grew closer together than usual, forming an almost solid clump of green. She concentrated her attention on it, and almost at once another flicker of motion appeared, followed by a third.

Jessie kept watching the area that had drawn her attention, and after a few moments she saw three riders emerge from the sheltering growth. They entered one of the little clearings that dotted the hills, and now she recognized Dan

178

Coats, then Will Talley. The third man was a stranger, but since he was riding almost stirrup to stirrup with Will Talley, she decided that the stranger must be Jim Talley, the assay-office superintendent.

As the trio rode closer and the angle between them and the balloon grew sharper, Jessie realized that the riders could not see the balloon. It would be hidden from them by their wide hat brims. They were leaning together in their saddles now, obviously talking to one another, unaware that they were being observed by Jessie from the basket of a balloon drifting silently overhead.

Jessie saw only the backs of the three men as they moved toward the road, but lost sight of them when they rode under the branches of the pines. After a few moments, Jim Talley emerged, riding alone. He continued across the road and disappeared into a clump of piñon trees. Jessie watched for a moment, but he did not go out on the other side of the grove.

She returned her attention to the opposite side of the road and saw Coats and Will Talley. She could get only an occasional glimpse of them, moving forms seen dimly below the screening pines.

Turning to Ted, she asked. "Can you stop us from going any higher? There are some men on the ground I'd like to watch for a few minutes."

"Sure. I'll just spill a little hot air out of the bag and we'll go down. Tell me when we're at the right altitude."

Putting the cover on the calcium chloride can, Ted pulled on the line that opened the exhaust panel on top of the air bag. The balloon began to drop slowly. Suddenly it swayed and spun around, and after a moment started to reverse the direction in which it had been moving.

"I'm sorry, Jessie," Ted said. "We're in the ground current now. It's going to carry us right back to the other side of the road unless I gain altitude again."

"Never mind," she told him. "This is the way I want to go for a few minutes. Dan Coats and Will Talley and another man are down there and I want to keep an eye on them."

"I'll do my best to hold us here, then," Ted promised. "If you'll tell me which way to go, I'll try to find the right current."

Jessie returned her attention to the road. She'd lost sight of Coats and Will Talley now, and Jim Talley was still out of sight. Then, as she looked along the road, she saw Ki for the first time. Realizing suddenly that he was heading for the place where the balloon had been launched, her quick instinct flashed her a warning signal.

Suddenly it was clear to Jessie why Dan Coats and the Talley brothers were waiting. She understood now why Jim Talley had ridden across the road, leaving his companions behind. She looked away from Ki long enough to inspect the treetops again, but wherever the ambushers were waiting, they were concealed by the branches of the trees.

Her voice urgent, she asked Ted, "Can you follow the road a little way without going any higher?"

"As long as the wind direction doesn't change, we'll be moving in the direction the road takes, but I can't guarantee we'll follow all its curves."

"That'll have to do, then," Jessie said without taking her eyes off Ki. He was steadily approaching the spot where Coats and his companions had stopped. "But it'd help if you could drop a little lower."

"I can't go down very much farther, Jessie. If we get too close to those treetops a gust of wind might push us into them."

"Take the risk," she said urgently. "If your balloon is

180

damaged or wrecked, I'll buy you another one.' '

Wishing desperately that she'd brought her rifle along, Jessie drew her Colt.

"What're you pulling that gun out for?" Ted asked, a puzzled frown creasing his face.

"If I'm right, Ki's about to be ambushed."

"Ambushed? Who's going to—"

"Dan Coats and Will Talley and his brother. It's too complicated to explain everything now, Ted, and I can't risk taking my eyes off the trees."

"You mean you can see them waiting down there for Ki?"

"I can't see them now, but I remember where they were when the trees started hiding them."

"It's funny I didn't see them, too," Ted said, frowning.

"You were busy working with the calcium chloride during the few minutes they were in sight. But they're there, all right, hiding under those trees."

"Do you think you can hit them with your pistol?"

"I can't even see them now, Ted. But I'm going to fire a shot or two into the place where I saw them last, more to warn Ki than with any hope of hitting the ones who're hiding."

"Can Ki fight back? I remember he doesn't carry a gun."

"Ki has his own ways of fighting, but they won't help him much at a time like this."

While she talked, Jessie had kept her eyes on the ground, trying to pick out the exact spot where she'd seen Coats and the Talleys disappear. Ki was on a curved section of the road now, out of her sight, but she knew he must be getting perilously close to the spot where the would-be assassins were hidden. She started to turn away and search the foliage once more, when out of the corner of her eye she saw Ki coming into sight around the curving section of the road.

Not daring to wait until Ki came closer, Jessie leaned out of the basket as far as she could and let off two quick shots into the treetops where she'd seen Coats and Will Talley disappear. Then she swiveled and got off another snap shot, aiming across the road at the area where Jim Talley had vanished.

Ki glanced up when he heard the shots. When he saw Jessie leaning out of the basket with her Colt in her hand he needed no other warning. With the skill and speed that his training had made almost instinctive, he launched himself from the saddle an instant before two rifles barked from the thick growth of piñons that bordered the road just ahead of him. Landing on his feet, Ki dived into the nearest thicket.

Standing in the basket, Jessie waited. Her eyes were fixed on the road, and she was aware that only two more shells were left in her Colt. She saw a stirring in the tops of the low-growing piñons that were clumped on the roadside near the spot where Ki had taken cover. The man Jessie had tagged as Jim Talley rode out. He was guiding his horse with his knees, his rifle in his hands rising to aim at the balloon.

Jessie brought up her revolver, but before either she or Talley could trigger off a shot, Ki rose from the thicket. Impelled by the steely muscles of his legs, his leap took him in an arc to the rump of Talley's horse. Talley's attention had been riveted on Jessie, and until Ki's feet landed on the horse's rump he was unaware of the danger behind him.

Ki landed with his hand poised to strike. Twisting his body to balance himself in his precarious position, he brought his right hand around in a short, powerful *tegatana-uchi* chop that struck Talley's nose just below the bridge. The steel-hard edge of Ki's palm shattered the delicate bones of Talley's nose and sent needle-sharp shards upward into his brain.

Talley died almost instantly. As his body lurched backward, Ki jumped free. A shot barked from the clump of piñon trees on the opposite side of the road, but Ki was already halfway to the ground before the slug whistled over the horse's back. Talley's limp form was still sliding to the ground when Ki dived off the road, where he'd landed on his feet, and rolled into the shelter of the shallow ledge at its edge.

A second rifle shot cracked, the bullet plowing into the roadside inches away from the spot where Ki had dropped to cover. The two rifle shots had given Jessie a target. Swiveling in the basket, she let off the last two rounds in her Colt. A cry of pain rose from the thicket. Jessie instinctively marked its source and raised her Colt again before realizing that she had only the cases of discharged shells in its cylinder. A second shot came from the thicket, this one from a heavier-caliber gun. The slug tore through the edge of the basket and into the bag.

Turning to Ted, Jessie asked, "Can you drop the balloon low enough for me to jump out?"

"I can try," he said. "But we may get hit again by whoever's shooting from those trees before we get to the ground."

"Try, then, and pray that they miss," she snapped.

"Be ready to jump just before we hit the ground," he said.

Yanking hard on the cord of the bleeder panel that let out the balloon's hot air, Ted stepped to the side of the basket. He grabbed the rim and flexed his legs as the balloon began dropping swiftly. The ground seemed to rush up

183

to meet them. Jessie gauged their fall and vaulted over the basket's side an instant before the balloon crashed.

She ran to the rifle Jim Talley had dropped, then quickly scooped it up, fell prone, and began pumping lead into the tangled huddle of low-growing piñons across the road. Another shot came from the thicket and Jessie replied to it, but when she worked the lever to pump another shot into the chamber and pulled the trigger, the click of the hammer told her that the magazine was empty.

Suddenly Jessie realized that no more shots had come from the piñon thicket. She waited, stretched motionless, but the only sound she heard was the faint sighing of the last vestiges of air escaping from the punctured bag.

"Ki?" Jessie called.

When Ki answered, his voice came from the opposite side of the road and Jessie realized that he'd used *ninja* tactics to cross to the other side unseen.

"I'm over here, Jessie!" he called. "And it's safe to stand up now. The shooting's over."

Unexpectedly, Ted spoke from behind Jessie. "I hope Ki's right. A gunfight was one thing I didn't look for."

Jessie was rising to her feet. Turning to face Ted, she said, "If Ki says it's safe, you can believe him."

Ted's eyes were fixed on the balloon. The bag still held enough air to support its domed top, but now it looked like a giant mushroom that had grown up to block the roadway.

"My balloon!" he said sadly.

"Don't worry," Jessie told him. "It was my fault that it got damaged. If it can't be fixed, I'll buy you another one."

Ki appeared around the sagging air bag. Jessie looked at him, her eyebrows lifting in a silent question. He nodded.

"Both of them," he said. "Coats was dead when I got

there, but Will Talley was going for his gun. I had to use a *shuriken* to stop him."

"Jessie, will you please tell me what this is all about?" Ted asked. "I feel like I've just gone through a small war."

"It's too long a story to go into now," Jessie said. "But as nearly as Ki and I could find out, the Talley brothers and Dan Coats have been stealing silver from the mine for quite a while. We caught up with them and were—well, we didn't expect it to end this way, but it's over now, and all that's left to do is clean up the pieces."

"Were you really serious when you said you'd buy me another balloon if this one's ruined?" he asked.

"Of course. And if you want to keep on looking—"

"No!" Ted interrupted. "I'll go back to giving exhibition ascensions at county fairs! To tell you the truth, Jessie, I think prospecting's a lot too dangerous. From now on, I'll be satisfied taking my chances on another levanter!"

Watch for

LONE STAR AND THE STAGECOACH WAR

fifty-third novel in the
exciting LONE STAR series from Jove

coming in January!